The Zambezi Chronicles:

Critical Fault

I0549095

A Novella by

Dwight Kopp

ISBN 978-0-9895853-3-0

On Facebook at www.facebook.com/dwightkoppbooks
On the web at www.dwightkopp.com

For Doe

Zambezi River Region

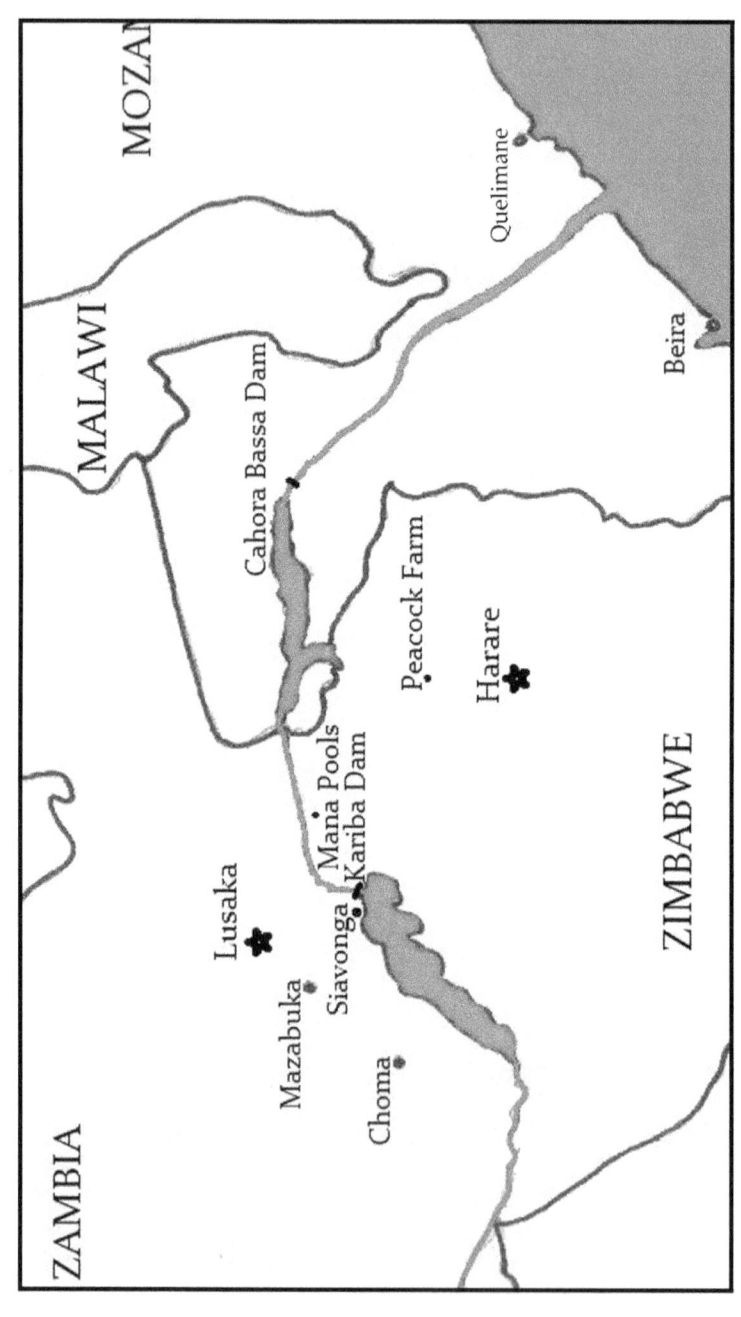

South Eastern Africa

Chapter 1
O'Hagan's Pub
Lusaka, Zambia
Thursday, March 11, 2007
6:00 p.m.

In O'Hagan's Pub three white men could blend in.

Stuart Hall's team found a discreet booth in the rear. Likely the only Irish pub in all of Zambia, O'Hagan's served customers in an upscale restaurant situated on the wing of the country's most popular strip mall. Other restaurants and gourmet cafés shared the same locale, offering a variety of foods to local and international clientele. The men would have preferred to sit on the wide tiled sidewalk under the shade of an umbrella for coffee and a pastry, but they knew word was out to find Daniel, and besides, it was raining. In spite of only eating camp food for the past few days, none of them were hungry.

"Gentlemen, let's make a plan." Stuart's face still looked drained. Somehow, he had to think like a soldier and not a father. "I think there is a way we can still pick our mango."

"Like hell, we can," Aaron said. "If we make any move to bag our fruit, our hopes of getting Sheila out are gone. You know Mpundu will be in touch with the head of the president's body guard right up until the time you guys come walking into his door."

Daniel Smith listened. His fingers traced patterns in the condensation on his cup.

"You are right," Stuart said. "But at this point, Mpundu does not know we are a party of three."

"What do you suggest?" Aaron Boll asked.

Stuart leaned forward and lowered his voice. "According to Mpundu's text, he wants Daniel in exchange for Sheila. Daniel is considered a threat to the president because of his connection to Gideon Chipinduka. The Mwanyisa government doesn't seem too concerned about my midnight departure from Zimbabwe, and either they haven't figured out I haven't signed over the title deed to the farm, or it doesn't matter to them. As long as they are in power, title deeds are a joke. For now, I am not in the center of their radar, and Aaron is not known. The odds are in our favor. Three against one." Stuart looked hard at Aaron. "You'll go to your spot as planned. Daniel and I will pay Mpundu a visit, rescue Sheila and show up if we can. After this, we'll have to separate." He motioned to Aaron. "You know where your ride and weapon are stored. We'll follow as soon as we find Sheila." Stuart waited for a waitress to pass out of earshot. "I don't have to tell you, Aaron, that your first shot matters. Hopefully, we can get into position in time to run our original plan."

Aaron shook his head. "Mpundu thinks Daniel is a threat to the president. What if you run into a snag, and I start shooting before you get Sheila?"

Stuart leaned back against the booth and looked at his son-in-law. "Sheila's life is already in danger. The first rule of guerilla warfare is this: Never make a deal with Satan. Never play by his rules. Even he won't honor them."

Stuart reached across the table and grabbed Aaron's forearm. "God go with you."

Aaron lit a cigarette and inhaled deeply. "I sure hope so."

Chapter 2
Cathedral d'Angelica
Venice, Italy

The sound of the boys' choir practice floated around stone columns supporting the vaulted ceiling. Ciro Michi lit a candle and placed it with the others. He dipped his fingers in the bronze bowl and crossed himself before entering the sanctuary. Michi walked softly down the aisle, the sole congregant in the provincial cathedral.

He had always loved church music.

Quietly, he whispered the prayer in Latin. "Ave Maria, gratia plena, Dominus tecum, benedicta tu in mulieribus…" He approached the statue of the blessed virgin at the front. Here he stood for a moment, studying the sculpture of the woman, masterfully carved in flawless marble.

Her eyes studied him from bowed head, as if he had interrupted a moment of private prayer. "Et benedictus fructus ventris tui, Iesus." Her outstretched hand drew him up the steps of the low altar. He stopped just before touching her. His old knees didn't work like they used to, and it took him a moment to kneel under her extended hand.

He bent low. Kissed her feet. The incense laden cold air echoed with a thousand years of whispered prayers.

"Holy Mary," he began, feeling the presence wrap around him. "Mother of God, pray for us sinners—."

Ethereal notes of the choir mixed with the voices of angels and Michi closed his eyes and let his mind wander. Here, at the feet of the Holy Mother, Ciro Michi could think without interruption from the evil one.

Arturo Esposito's plan had failed. Michi would certainly have heard news of the dam's failure, but instead, broadcasts had been dominated by the banal discourse of local politicians vying for position. Michi snorted in disgust. The local election was already decided. He had sordid information about both men and would use it well. Matters of this importance could not be left to chance. It was, after all, Michi's holy duty to steer the course of human events.

Why else would he have been given the power to do so?

Michi invested heavily in emerging South American copper markets. The temporary elimination of Zambia's major mining operation would have been a windfall, and he banked heavily on the plan's success. He had thrown almost everything he had behind Esposito's plan, but the hydroelectric dam remained intact and his valuable assets rendered unavailable.

Michi looked into the face of the Holy Mother. "He has failed me."

Chapter 3
Lusaka, Zambia
Friday
11:15 a.m.

Throngs of laughing, singing and sweating people pressed into Lusaka's fair grounds to catch a glimpse of their continent's leaders. The President of Zambia, Nigel Tawona, presided over the assembly of Heads of State and other dignitaries. The Heads sat behind him, facing reporters and cameras in the sweltering heat. Public life had its costs after all.

President Tawona stood before the microphone and looked out on his people. "Before you are gathered leaders representing the entire southern half of the continent of Africa and the Indian Ocean. We have come together today to pledge to you, the constituents, our unflagging commitment to bring Africa together."

Cameras flashed. Tawona wryly noted the two foreign reporters. International media didn't care about Africa unless there was a disaster. It mattered little to Towana, but the world needed a different conception of Africa. Something more than images of poverty, tribal violence and bloodshed that dominated Western appetites.

"We pledge, as member states of the Southern African Development Community, to move forward economically, socially and politically in a coordinated community of member nations. It is our determined purpose, to leverage our cooperation to the greatest advantage. While much of Africa is falling into ruin, we have taken our spears and beaten them into plow shares. The spear has never given jobs to the people. People cannot eat the fruit of violence." Several heads of state nodded sagely behind him and a few cast sidelong glances at Zimbabwe's President Mwanyisa, the only dictator represented.

Towana continued. "We cannot forsake our dignity by letting Western nations dictate Africa's political and social direction with their aid. We must cultivate healthy international partnerships to bring true development in conjunction with the morals, aims and directives of our people."

He turned and acknowledged the men behind him. "On behalf of the people of Southern Africa and the Islands of the Indian Ocean, I charge you leaders to faithfully discharge the full duties of your posts in the days ahead.

"And on behalf of the people of my country, welcome to Zambia."

Teams of drummers decked out in matching white t-shirts filled the air with sound. Applause swelled around the platform. Ululations rose above the noise. Security personnel patrolled the roped-off area.

Cars snaked off behind the stage in the prescribed order. The presidential vehicles, shipped in for the occasion from their respective countries, stood polished, ready and air conditioned. The Heads of State pretended not to hurry. They waved and smiled and shook hands for the cameras.

Mwanyisa climbed into the Rolls Royce and felt the rush of cool air. But even with the heat, he welcomed the coat and tie. The feel of power. He leaned forward. Wanted the black sea of cheering faces to see him. Accolades. He nodded and smiled and felt the magic.

Tandem white motorcycles with blue lights led the motorcade, sirens blaring. Three blue police cars followed behind. The line of vehicles carrying Africa's royalty waited to exit the parade grounds.

Chapter 4
Lusaka, Zambia
Parking Lot of the Manda Hill Shopping Centre
11:29 a.m.

Enoch Mpundu sat in the white Land Cruiser and watched his mirrors. Two grenades hung from his belt, partially hidden by his shirt.

He left the truck running and the air conditioning on. The woman, covered in a traditional burqa, sat still beside him. She had been difficult, but he eventually 'convinced' her to come along. It helped that his assistant found her brother, the taxi driver. If she complied, he told her, her brother might live. He didn't have time to look for the white woman. He hoped the ruse would work long enough to make the trade.

"When the man comes to the door, I will instruct him to open it. You will exit without speaking. If you do not follow my directions, I will cut out your brother's tongue before I kill him."

She said nothing, immobile under the black burqa.

There just had not been enough time to find the white woman. He had her phone and one of his men was guarding the house in case she came back. He knew he was running out of time. The burqa presented an almost perfect solution. Unfortunately, there were few women who wore full burqas in Zambia, and the novelty drew a few stares as people passed their parked vehicle. Daniel only had to believe the woman was Sheila long enough for Mpundu to kill him.

Across the street, the parade ground echoed with the sound of drums and people cheering. Mpundu followed along on live radio coverage of the event.

Mpundu's phone chimed. "Yes?"

"The motorcade will soon be underway," the voice reported.

Mpundu had counted on it being late. Since when did a head of state complete a speech on time? President Nigel Tawona was the first.

Bloody hell, Mpundu thought. Daniel must be in hand before Mwanyisa joined the procession. Once they started through town, security would prove more difficult. The rest of Mwanyisa's security detail questioned Mpundu's ability to deal with the threat, but Mpundu insisted. It was a matter of pride. White men would give almost anything for their women. Still, if the security detail didn't receive word that the threat was neutralized, they would pull Mwanyisa from the procession. For his part, Mpundu cared little about the parade, but the dictator made it clear that the people wanted to see him, and he would be upset if Mpundu failed to keep that option open.

A parking lot security guard stood beside his door and knocked on the window. "Can I help you, sir?"

Where had he come from? Mpundu cracked the window. "No thank you. I'm just listening to the radio. It is too crowded over there." He motioned to the parade ground across the street.

The guard moved off, gawking at the woman made invisible under the drapery of cloth. He disappeared into one of the enclosed guard-towers in the parking lot.

The reporter announced the Heads of State as they entered their vehicles for the motorcade. Mpundu was out of time. He could hear the drums and cheering grow louder as the big men started to move.

Mwanyisa could not be disappointed. He dialed the dictator's phone. Mwanyisa would be less likely to ask for specifics than the security detail.

Mpundu spoke into the receiver. "I have him." It was a calculated lie. "You can proceed." The dictator listened and clicked off without a word. Now Mpundu must not fail.

#

Crowds close to the road jumped with excitement. Inside the presidential vehicle, Mwanyisa relished the throbbing drums and cheering people. Here and there white faces intermingled with black. One grand audience. Traditional dress mixed into the mélange of young people in blue jeans reaching over barriers to snap pictures with their cell phones. Troops of women danced ahead of the motorcade.

Mwanyisa's secret service surrounded the vehicle, halting the driver.

The dictator cracked his window to a soldier hired from Iran's elite special-forces. The intensity of the cheering and music doubled with the window open. Mwanyisa smiled and looked past the soldier to the people.

"Mr. President. Our threat has not been neutralized. Please order your driver to exit the parade ground to the right for a secure escort. There a helicopter will take you to the hotel."

"The people must see me." Mwanyisa was firm.

"Mr. President, there is no way we can guarantee your safety through the city."

The president's phone buzzed. He put it to his ear to listen, snapped it shut and turned back to the soldier.

9

"That was Mpundu. I am going," He reached forward and tapped his driver on the shoulder. "Go on. We are delaying the procession."

His driver pulled the silver Rolls-Royce out of the parade ground and took his place behind the president of Malawi. They were seventh in the motorcade.

#

Enoch Mpundu turned to the woman beside him. "Remember your brother. If you fail, he will die, and I will hunt down his family. You will do exactly as instructed." He scanned the parking lot again and re-checked his mirrors. The waiting was beginning to wear. What if the white man decided to leave the woman? What if she had contacted him already?

"You are a coward." Annie said.

Enoch gave a snort.

She moved under the burqa, reached out and placed a metal grenade pin on his knee.

For a moment he stared at it uncomprehending. His hands groped the string of grenades on his belt. One was missing.

"If you release the trigger you will die," he said. Already he was working to disconnect his seatbelt.

"Inshallah." As God wills, she replied. "Go to hell."

Too late, Enoch realized his mistake. His hands pulled at the latch, tearing at the locked door. He felt the flash and saw glass from the Land Cruiser explode out into the parking lot before the concussive force of blast and fire pressed him into darkness.

Chapter 5
Manda Hill Shopping Center
Lusaka, Zambia

Stuart bartered with a security guard for rights to use the lookout post. The elevated guard shacks positioned at strategic places throughout the mall parking lot gave patrons a sense of security. The towers, just high enough to peer over the top of vehicles, had been colorfully painted as a concession against the prison look. About the size of a hunting blind, the guard shacks were accessed via a ladder underneath. A single guard could sit in the dark interior and have a 360-degree view of the surrounding area through a six-inch gap that ran the perimeter of the hide just beneath its tin roof. Designed by some security outfit in South Africa, they afforded parking lot guards the luxury of seeing out without being easily seen.

At exactly 10:30 a.m. Daniel received a text message from Sheila's phone indicating the location for the trade. Stuart and Daniel had little time to work up a plan, but at least they were familiar with the place. Using a passing vehicle to screen him from view, Stuart ascended the ladder to the guard shack. He disappeared into the shadowy inside around 11:20 a.m. Using the scope from his rifle, he located Mpundu and Sheila within minutes and called in their location.

Across the road, the drummers started and the sound drifted easily to the shopping center. In a few minutes, the presidential procession would be under way.

From his vantage point, Stuart could also see Daniel situated on the terraced café outside the coffee shop. Stuart pressed the phone to his ear. "I have them in sight." He clicked the scope into place, locked the butt of the Styer back into position, and chambered a round.

"Is she okay?" Daniel asked.

"It is hard to say. There is a glare on the window."

"Am I in his line of sight?"

"Negative. Get your motorbike," Stuart said.

Daniel fitted the earpiece of his cell into place and walked to his motorbike.

"Wait." It was Stuart. "A guard is approaching the car. I can't take Mpundu out yet, and there is traffic coming. I'll have them out of sight for a few seconds."

Stuart cursed under his breath as the blue taxi van stopped to discharge a group of older women carrying full plastic bags. It took them some time getting out. When it moved on, the guard had left Mpundu's truck.

"It's a go. You have exactly one minute on my mark." Stuart pinned the rifle in his neck to check his watch. "Ready. Mark."

The stopwatch beeped. It would only take Daniel a few seconds to navigate through the crowd to Mpundu's vehicle and Sheila. He needed to arrive just after the shot to get Sheila out of there and away from the scene. They did not want to get tied up in an investigation. Time was critical.

Stuart placed the cross hairs of his gun sight directly on Mpundu's forehead. The angle of fire would send the bullet through his head toward the rear of the vehicle. He steadied his nerves. Mpundu moved.

"What are you doing, you bastard?" Stuart whispered. He was painfully aware of the sound of the motorcade beginning to set out behind him. They needed to get into position to help Aaron—

Fire and glass erupted from Mpundu's vehicle, the flash of light illuminating the inside of Stuart's hide. Vibration from the grenade shook the metal sides of the guard shack. "O God—"

"What happened?" Daniel heard it, too.

Stuart slumped to the floor. Bits of burning debris fell from the sky; clattered on the tin roof. Below people scattered; running away from the explosion.

Chapter 6
Near the Great North Road
Lusaka, Zambia

Aaron steered his motorbike along the edge of the rutted road. Recent rains filled the depressions. The shantytown sprawled out from center city. Vendors erected kiosks close enough that a person could reach out his car window to purchase wares. The stalls were constructed from long poles cut from trees and tied together with bark rope. Crude shelves were covered with bags of salt, corn meal, and bottles of every conceivable shape or size filled with cooking oil.

A narrow path ran between merchants' stalls and rough, mud brick houses topped with rusting corrugated iron and black plastic. The chatter of pedestrians and the rasp of tired boom boxes pumping out township music usually filled this section of town. But today, the ding of a solitary bicycle bell was all Aaron heard when he cut the engine and backed his ride onto a path cut between two houses. The bicyclist hurried to take his place with the crowd one block over. Already the people pressed together against the temporary barriers erected by police along the parade route. Aaron pulled the key and followed the foot path.

A grey cinderblock wall defined the perimeter of the freight company's dispatch center. He walked around to the side. Broken glass topped the wall, but a section next to the tree had been cleared. He wasn't the first person to climb in here. Likely the shantytown kids came after dark to play in the shadows and pretend they were driving the huge trucks. If the kids could get in, they must be able to get out. As yet, Aaron wasn't sure if he could find a way back over the wall. He had a set of bolt cutters in his pack, but trails like that can be followed.

Aaron could hear the cheering crowds. Groups of drummers and dancing women would lead the procession of dignitaries until they reached the northern limit of town where the parade would end. Timing had been discussed at length. Too soon and the neighborhood would be crowded. Too late and he'd miss his chance for a clear shot.

He dropped to the ground inside the wall and glanced around. His cover story was that he was a photographer for the London Times, and he needed a good spot for a picture. The pathetic ruse required he carry a camera. But good cover stories were hard to come by. Especially for white guys who climbed on top of someone else's truck in broad daylight intending to shoot a president.

The trailer sat along the sidewall of the truck compound. Aaron shouldered his bag and climbed the rear ladder rails. The roof of the trailer creaked when he belly crawled into position. He kept as low as possible. The position afforded him one line of sight through tattered back yards to the paved road in the distance. The firing line followed the makeshift alley between houses linking the lane where he parked with the main tar road, which ran parallel to it. A few clothes left hanging on lines interfered with his view, but he would have to make do. The crowd filled the gap by the road. He would just have enough height to get a clear shot over their heads.

Depending on the speed of the motorcade, Aaron would have ten seconds to change the course of history. It was going to be close. He tried not to think. Tried to remember he was the good guy. Tried not to feel foolish, and guilty and illegitimate.

Aaron unzipped the pack. Holding the rifle helped. He swung the hinged stock into position; listened to it click into place. He chambered the first round and flicked off the safety.

Chapter 7
Manda Hill Mall
Lusaka, Zambia

Stuart caught Daniel just before his son-in-law reached the blaze and pushed him hard against a car. "You can't go over there."

"Like hell I can't," Daniel said, pushing back.

Stuart's muscles knotted to keep Daniel still. Black smoke boiled from the burning wreck. "She's gone, Danny. There's nothing we can do for her. There's nothing to see. It's over."

The young man sagged to the ground, his face buried in his hand.

Stuart stood next to him knuckling tears from his own eyes.

Once the debris stopped falling, people rushed toward the wreckage. Someone found a fire extinguisher. Car alarms blared around the blast site and mall security called for fire trucks that would never come.

Stuart left Daniel and walked toward the wreck. Shopkeepers and pedestrians squinted at the heat. What happened? Stuart shoved down the grief threatening to break over him. He couldn't look at the fire. It was unthinkable. His only daughter.

Stop, he told himself. Later. But the 'later' threatened to overwhelm him now. He averted his eyes from the passenger seat.

He felt a hand on his shoulder and turned.

Daniel stood beside him; his hollow eyes stared uncomprehending at the derelict SUV.

"It is time to go," Daniel said.

Stuart shot him a surprised look.

"I'm going to kill the bastard responsible for this," Daniel said.

"I don't think we have enough time." Stuart glanced at his watch.

"Maybe," Daniel said, "but I have nothing more to lose." Daniel turned and hurried off.

Stuart called after him. "Don't forget your earphone."

#

The dignitaries and celebrants passed the roundabout at the north end of town, past the copper statue of a fish eagle reaching for its prey. Cairo Road had been closed off to give the parade right of way.

Mwanyisa's phone buzzed again, but he ignored it. This was his moment. Perhaps he could be the President of Zambia as well. The countries had once been linked by colonial rule. He could link them again. Access to Iran's weapons technology made the possibility appealing to him. It only surprised him he had not thought of it sooner.

He waved to the cheering crowd. My people, he thought.

#

Three blocks north, Stuart and Daniel scrambled into position, made radio contact with Aaron and tried to settle their breathing. They did not discuss the Manda Hill incident. Stuart positioned himself in a sugar gum tree behind the secondary school, and Daniel lay atop a low roof. Just in time. The first sleek black vehicle crawled through their cross hairs. They waited. Counted off the cars. Pushed away tears that blurred vision.

17

"Just like rehearsal, boys. On my mark." Stuart's voice sounded choked, but they heard him clearly through their earpieces over the throb of drums and the clamor of people.

He waited for the signal from the other men.

"Daniel is clear."

Aaron would be next to see Mwanyisa's vehicle. Stuart would be the last.

"What are you doing there?" Stuart jumped. A boy stood below, staring up at him. He realized the boy couldn't see his rifle lying on top of the tree limb.

"Even big boys like to climb trees. Now run along and see what you can see. You're almost too late." The boy smiled and waved and sprinted toward the crowd, obviously trying to show off.

Mwanyisa's vehicle crawled forward.

Another voice cut through their concentration. "Aaron is clear."

Stuart spoke into the radio. "Ready." Chamber a round. A breath. Exhale. Mark target. Ticking off the mental checklist.

"Aim." Rifle stocks pressed against their cheeks. Safety off. Just like rehearsal.

At last the president's vehicle came into Stuart's field of view.

"Fire."

Glass spidered on the windows; Mwanyisa fell back in his seat. Secret service agents moved to cover him from all sides. Stuart's voice repeated the series. "Ready. Aim. Fire." Just like their practice in the Lochinvar Game Reserve.

The report of their rifles disappeared in the din of the parade.

Chapter 8
Kariba Dam
Friday, March 12
11:39 a.m.

Manfred Mwata leaned against the commemorative plaque fastened to the concrete barrier. The barrier followed the road across the top of the Kariba Dam. He pressed a handheld radio to his ear, trying to hear Michael Jackson through the static.

Rain fell all night and the still-gray sky pressed down over the lake. Not that he minded a break from the heat, but his green rain parka felt sticky and his stomach growled. Mwata squinted at his wristwatch. The glass fogged up making the face difficult to read. Almost lunch time.

He pushed off his leaning post, adjusted the green webbed shoulder strap of his machine gun, and walked down the glistening sidewalk. Since the festivities of the dam's flood gates opening, nothing had happened. The near complete absence of traffic turned his job back into a boring vigil with nothing to watch. He sang along with Jackson. Thankfully, payday was Friday. Tonight he would eat fish, buy some cigarettes and —

Mwata blinked hard, suddenly unsteady. He reached to take hold of the concrete guardrail. The wall moved.

A great yawning sound moaned out from beneath him. To his right a spray of water jetted from the dam face. The fan grew as he watched, spreading like the tail of a massive peacock.

The soldier lost his balance, lurched and fell hard against the rail. His weapon strap slipped from his shoulder; the radio clattered against concrete. His mind raced to keep up. Beneath him the wall swung open like a gate, accompanied by a great roar Mwata thought came from the river itself. The sidewalk pivoted violently, shifting away from the lake. Mwata's knees felt rubbery; he could not make them move.

The dam crumbled, mammoth chunks of concrete gave way under the immeasurable pressure of the reservoir.

Mwata fell, rigid as a tin soldier knocked from a shelf. A thunderous crack erupted from the dam, the wall ruptured and disappeared entirely, brushed aside by the mighty power of the river god. Blocks the size of buildings crushed the power stations beneath even before water obliterated them from view. The concrete detritus scoured the gorge, propelled along by the weight of 186 billion cubic meters of water.

The Kariba surged like a drunkard, tumbled over its own feet and fell again, raging ever forward. It clawed past the tattered edges of its restraint, stripping the ground to naked bedrock. The savage, thrusting cascade flashed down the Kariba Gorge at speeds up to 60 miles per hour. Concrete chunks of the wall floated impossibly in the torrent. Hundreds of trees, like knickknacks in a vortex, emerged and disappeared again in snarling foam.

The river rushed onward to the sea over 1,000 miles away.

Africa would never be the same.

Chapter 9
Lusaka, Zambia
Friday, March 12

Four dun colored choppers flashed black shadows across bare ground; gunners hung from open doors and the whack and thump of rotors pressed back branches of nearby trees. Netcare 911 Medevac Unit One flew in just behind her military escort. Dust and people scattered as the yellow Medevac's landing skids touched down in front of the secondary school.

Zambia's Special Forces made a perimeter; emergency crews rushed forward. The secret service already had the dictator out of the vehicle. Blood stained the old man's shirt and vest.

"He's still alive." A secret service agent yelled above the roar of the chopper.

The medic team lifted the man onto a stretcher, fastened a safety belt across his legs and hustled him to the open bay.

They secured the stretcher as the chopper lifted off. The tail rotor spun around—shearing leaves from a nearby tree—and pulled away, skimming low over the rooftops for the short flight back to the airport and the waiting medevac jet.

The South African Netcare Medevac team ran the most sophisticated medical evacuation unit in the southern hemisphere. Their regular doctor, however, had been given the day off. The Zambian government supplied his replacement.

One of the medics shouted, "He is still breathing, doctor, but his vital signs aren't good."

The doctor put a hand on the medic's shoulder, leaned close to the medic's ear and replied. "Where a man is fighting for life there are no titles. Please, call me Gideon."

The air control tower at Lusaka International Airport pre-cleared the chopper. It settled onto the grass at the end of the runway next to Medevac Unit Two. The engines of the corporate jet already whined and her pilots scrambled through preflight. Unit Two medics assisted in transferring the patient. The jet started rolling before the cabin door closed. Every second mattered. Monitor lights flashed as the team worked to stabilize Mwanyisa. The whine of the jet's duct fan filled the cabin and the plane screamed down the runway.

Dr. Gideon Chipinduka settled himself to oversee the patient during the flight to Johannesburg where the most advanced surgical team on the continent would be waiting.

Chapter 10
Flood Refugee Camp
Southeastern Zambia
Friday, March 12

Zambia, Zimbabwe, Malawi and Mozambique all followed strict evacuation protocols in the days before the scheduled release at Kariba Dam. Masses of people were pressed into refugee facilities all along the Zambezi. The World Health Organization and UNICEF assisted the governments. Most evacuees were subsistence farmers and their worn, mismatched clothing clashed with the too-clean plastic and canvas supplied for the occasion by the Red Cross.

Gift walked to the edge of camp where older boys kicked a pink football they'd been given by one of the WHO staff. Sticks pressed into the ground marked goals and the barefoot boys imagined themselves playing for the World Cup.

Gift passed them and walked a short distance to a place where she could see down to the river. *The river has always been my friend.* She heard her father's voice. Gift squinted at the river and the overcast sky. The river had swollen high above its banks, even higher than the officials said it would after the flood gates had been opened. Gift knew her mother and brother's graves were gone now, swallowed up. Maybe she should pray to the river—they were all in the river now.

Not a single bird hopped among the branches of the trees. Strange, she thought. Maybe they, too, have had to move. But why, she wondered. People said the water would not come any higher.

A whisper of breeze pulled through the leaves. She could feel it. Something important was about to happen. She knew the feeling.

Had known it before her mother died. Known it before brother fell into the fire. She had known it before the lorries arrived to take them away from the village.

Maybe her father had just died. The thought made her eyes sting.

Sounds of cheering drifted back to her from the boys at the camp. Father had always been good at football. She remembered watching him play with the others on Independence Day when teachers and parents squared off against the students at the local school.

She had been so proud when he scored. She danced and sang a little song for him from the sidelines. Mother had been too weak to come. Gift blinked at the memory.

She squatted down and cupped her face in her hands. The calling boys drifted back to her and, here and there on the wind, the sound of people talking or the distant chatter of radio. These faded in and out, but something was missing.

It was the insects, she realized. They were too quiet. The insects had stopped speaking.

Dogs howled back at camp. All of them. A snake slipped past, uncaring.

Thunder rumbled from the ground and she felt a curious movement beneath her feet.

Gift noticed the chill on her neck; the breeze changed direction. Birds of all varieties, silent and invisible before, flushed from the trees and joined a cacophonic swarm. Falcons, songbirds and buzzards, oblivious to each other, amassed in one chaotic swirl of movement.

The ground shuddered. Upstream, the barrage of a hundred thousand hooves pounded the earth. At first, Gift thought it was cattle stampeding, but the incomprehensible blur of animals moved among the trees. She knuckled tears from her eyes, tried to make it out. Another sound filled the air, the sound of the river gasping for breath.

She stood unmoving, bewildered and uncomprehending. The grasping wall over one hundred meters high, stumbling and falling in its haste, raged down the sides of the Kariba Gorge. The boiling savage, thrashed its teeth—clawing, scrambling forward, and tumbled again.

So, she thought, the river has come for me as well. Trancelike, she walked toward the moving mountain as it descended on her.

The deluge surged, pitching and bucking against the constraints of the hills on either side, ravishing the bush, and stripping the valley to its bones.

Gift disappeared under the writhing, murky snarl of the river god. The front of water did not advance at a set pace, but staggered against the net of debris caught up in its maw. When it breached, terrific jets of water erupted forward to be trampled again as it gathered speed and fury.

Chapter 11
Office of the President
Lusaka, Zambia
Friday, March 12
12:30 p.m.

Davison Chuma slid a single sheet of paper across the desk to the president's personal assistant. "Here is the press release. It has already been authorized."

The assistant pushed on his glasses and read the statement. He opened his laptop and copied the release in an email to the BBC, London Office:

At 11:45 today, a rogue international terrorist unit attempted to assassinate Zimbabwe's long time president, Cedric Mwanyisa, during a parade of Southern African Heads of State. Zambia's military pursued the assailants and intercepted them on the outskirts of Lusaka. The terrorists opened fire but were subsequently killed in the ensuing fight. In order to preserve the integrity of their investigation, Zambian officials can release no further details at this time.

The assistant clicked send and the power blinked. The lights went out, leaving the room in cool shadows. A warning bell sounded and the battery icon appeared indicating the loss of external power.

Chapter 12
Chirundu, Zambia
Friday, March 12

Hemmed in by hills on either side, the cataclysmic press of water forced its way forward. Villages and towns in the valley disappeared—erased as cleanly as if they had never been. The black and gray fury of water advanced on Chirundu. Within fifteen seconds, the entire city vanished. Bridges, shops, schools, government offices, trees. Gone. There had been no warning. Roads leading to the city from the highlands ended abruptly, as if the builders merely decided to give up. Telephone and electric lines snapped and dangled from poles on the hill overlooking the deluge.

Arturo Esposito's hopes that reporters covering the refugee camps would capture his moment failed miserably. The temporary camps of displaced people with the reporters simply ceased to exist.

The Kafue River, feeding the Zambezi downstream of Kariba Dam, flowed backward, over-flooding its banks far into the Kafue National Park, sweeping up herds of startled elephant and antelope.

And so it was for every city and town and village and farm that pressed itself close to the Zambezi's life-giving water. Mighty Nyaminyami, the river god, exacted his revenge.

Water imprisoned by the highlands thundered east. There it broke from the constraints of the Kariba Gorge Valley, accelerating to over sixty miles per hour.

The long pressure of water along the east branch of the Great Rift fault line disappeared. The earth arched her back to recover from the strain, heaving and stretching as if waking from a long slumber. Earthquakes registered along the Rift as far north as Ethiopia. A seismograph recorded 6.3 in Bujumbura, Burundi, over one thousand miles away.

The river god was not finished.

Less than three hours later, the deluge reached the western end of the Cahora Bassa Reservoir. Around 2:30 p.m., all communication from the town of Feira ceased. Zumbo fell silent.

But no one was listening.

The flood slowed briefly overspreading the Cohra Bassa reservoir, effectively swallowing the coastal towns of Mague and Chicoa. Rivers feeding Africa's fourth largest man-made lake flooded backward, washing away hundreds of villages.

The 180.6 cubic kilometers of water from Kariba pressed forward. The combined reserves of the Kariba and Cahora Bassa conspired together for the worst natural disaster Africa ever faced. Under the incalculable mass, tectonic plates shifted again, triggering seismographic monitoring stations throughout the Southern Hemisphere.

The Cahora Bassa Dam had survived decades of civil war. Standing five hundred sixty feet off the valley floor and spanning almost one thousand feet at its rim, it had been built to rival the Kariba. But the water gathered strength, flashing overtop, ripped away the dam's footing and destroyed the last obstacle. The Zambezi River could now finish its rampage to the sea, three hundred miles to the South East.

Chapter 13
Fairchild Physical Sciences Center
Dartmouth College, New Hampshire

Professor Morray parked and hung his wife's blue handicap sign from the rear view mirror. She wouldn't mind. She got the house and the mortgage and the dog. He got the orange 1954 Chevy pickup, the golf cart and the handicap tag she forgot to take with her. Across the street, the weathervane on the steeple fingered the North-West. The brilliant white columns of the United Church of Christ made the day feel warmer than it was. Cheery, even. Until he opened the door. Wind followed the Connecticut River.

Morray pulled a cap over his head and ducked into the Fairchild Physical Science Center.

The Dartmouth Flood Observatory was Morray's baby. He'd worked hard to sell the project to just the right people and managed enough initial grant money to be taken seriously. Dartmouth's own reputation hadn't hurt. Morray partnered with the European Commission's Global Disaster Alert and Coordination System and ITHACA—the Information Technology for Humanitarian Assistance, Cooperation and Action headquartered in Torino, Italy. He even collaborated with the United Nations International Strategy for Disaster Reduction. Heady stuff.

The Flood Observatory subscribed to First Look, a data package available from Digital Globe. The data came from a payload on two satellites in low earth, sun-synchronous, polar orbits. The Modis 250 package onboard the Aqua and Tera provided a whole new way to track seasonal fluctuations in surface water. The algorithms Morray created to manipulate the data gave emergency response and preparedness teams access not only to near real time data, but also made projections based on regional topography and weather forecasts. His 'baby' had been responsible for a measure of international notoriety.

Suddenly everyone wanted him. Emergency logistic managers, insurance companies, other universities. Everyone except his wife. He'd lost her and gained the whole world. At least that was how he looked at it. Not a bad trade, but he missed the dog.

Although the Dartmouth Flood Observatory computers ran all the time, digesting data forwarded from the satellite control stations, few students came in early. Morray didn't mind. It gave him time to brew coffee, ignore his email and study the previous night's data without interruption.

Li Lau didn't get the 'sleep-in' memo. She practically ran over him when she burst from the lab waving several sheets of paper. She'd told him that Li meant 'beautiful.' And she was. He was old, but he wasn't dead. Still, it wasn't her slender figure that caught his attention, but her breathless excitement. She'd found something.

Li babbled on in Mandarin. She did that when she got excited. It sometimes took her a while to realize what she was doing. Morray usually pretended to follow along until she caught the twitch of a smile and switched back to English.

But this time, Li's excitement had more in it. Something she didn't need to translate.

Fear.

From their lab they could watch the world like gods. They spent the days comparing one day's data against their growing collection. Watching oceans birth great storms; watching monsoons sweep across south Asia, watching regional flooding spring up after passing hurricanes. Floods showed as red overlays on black rivers. They could watch, but they could do very little.

The Dartmouth Flood Observatory provided a front row seat for natural disasters. The information was useful, life-saving in some cases. Most of the time, they just watched red smears indicating seasonal flooding, listened to their music and tried not to think about the people whose lives were washed away.

Morray forgot about the coffee and scanned the printouts. He recognized the signature of the Zambezi River, spawned somewhere in the dark interior of the northwestern corner of Zambia. He double checked the date. They'd been monitoring the scheduled opening of the Kariba Dam floodgates to alleviate abnormally high seasonal rains, but this couldn't be right. He double checked the dates on the image.

Li fell silent as he shuffled through the papers, comparing the new pictures against the baseline which he already had memorized.

The satellite captured a massive smear snaking almost eight hundred miles across the continent. It was moving fast. Too fast. The growing red scar crossed the continent below the equator and above the Tropic of Capricorn.

Morray glanced at his watch. This was happening right now. Gooseflesh crawled up his arms. He looked at Li, still uncomprehending. Li's dark eyes left no doubt. This was for real.

Morray started running.

Chapter 14
Zambezi River Area

As the sun began to set, satellites recorded the flickering attempts of the region's power grid coping with systemic failure. Zambia, Zimbabwe, Mozambique, and a portion of northern South Africa went dark. Here and there light appeared, only to fade again as the region's infrastructural machinery staggered along under an increased load.

The black water continued its journey, rushing ever-faster as the ground fell away before it.

Power was already out in Tete, one hundred miles southeast of Cahora Bassa when dam authorities issued bizarre, initial reports about Kariba. People with access to battery-operated radios gave the news little consideration. The Kariba Dam was, after all, over five hundred miles away.

First Tete and Bandar, then Chiramba and Chemba all washed away as completely as a child sweeps aside a town in his sandbox. And the water plunged toward the sea.

Further downstream, the mysterious reports created mass chaos in places and arrogant dismissals in others. But it mattered little. The torrents swept away the panicking and the unbelieving alike.

Those in Mozambique, like Sena and Mutarara and points south had more time. Almost two hundred miles from Tete, officials with megaphones alerted a few residential areas. Masses of people filled the streets, trampling underfoot thousands of the weak, slow and unlucky.

Some fled in vehicles, but roads often follow valleys.

The flood took them all.

Too late, vague evacuation and flood warnings reached the sleeping river population centers in lower Mozambique and coastal towns from Quelimane to Beira.

After consuming Sena and Mtarara, the water escaped the crowding valley and flung its arms wide. There, the inundation separated, forcing a southern channel behind Monte Nhamalongo. Surrounding the few hills of Gorongosa National Park, water engulfed the Pungwe River to devour Beira, Mozambique, a city of over half a million people. The water pounded already saturated coastal towns scraping them from the map and removing islands that stood as gatekeepers to the mouth of the Great Zambezi River.

News wires across the globe scrambled leading headlines. Something interesting was finally happening in Africa besides tribal war, ethnic cleansing and AIDS.

Producers called scientists; projections were made.

At last the world took notice.

The Regional Tsunami Service Providers, established by UNESCO, activated alarms on the Islands of the Indian Ocean. Those who heard it scrambled to higher ground.

Three thousand miles away, Perth, Australia and other western facing coastal cities initiated evacuation procedures.

Three hundred miles into the Mozambique Channel, luxury yachts and sailing vessels exploring the corals of Bassas de India and Europa received the mayday from both Malagasy and South African Coast Guards. Container ships bound for all ports from Durban, South Africa to Port Gentil, Gabon acknowledged the alert. On board, sailors donned life vests and captains stood watch at the helm, binoculars pressed up against the glass in horrid fascination.

Super-charged with debris and humanity from one thousand miles and fed by the press of seasonal rains, the two hundred fifty cubic kilometers of water crashed into the sea. The shock spawned tsunamis that swamped seaside communities in Madagascar from Antisiranana in the north to Betanty in the south.

Newscasters, numbed by the magnitude of the disaster sat and stared with the world at satellite photos and video feeds beginning to make their way out.

Casualty estimates climbed by the millions. By comparison, the Christmas tsunami of 2004 was a hiccough.

For Africa, the great tribulation had begun.

Chapter 15
Lusaka, Zambia

Sheila crept from the sweltering attic. Night had fallen. There had been gunshots in the house. The whole house listened. Enoch Mpundu told his man to stay behind. Her whole body ached with fatigue and the strain from perching on the joists. Thirst had driven her to venture out from her hiding place.

She crawled down from the bureau beneath the access panel and sat on the edge of the bed, rubbing aching muscles. The rough boards cut into her forearms and legs, but the thirst and the unknown were the worst.

She rifled through her suitcase for a pair of shorts and shoes. Then she grabbed her handbag and slipped down the dark hallway. Nothing else moved. Ears strained against the darkened silence. She found the kitchen, cupped her hand under the faucet and drank greedily.

For a moment she didn't care if someone did find her, so long as they let her finish drinking. She wiped her mouth and stared out the kitchen window. The low hanging moon rested just above the garden's walls, but not a single light burned on the property or around it.

Nothing made a sound. Where were her hosts? Long hours in the attic had given her plenty of time to think and worry about Daniel. She had tried to remember why she had walked out on him, but the reasons sounded hollow.

Sheila walked down the hall toward Annie's bedroom. She peered through the open door. A veil of moonlight draped across someone in the bed.

"Annie?" Sheila crept forward, smelled blood and stopped short. "Oh God." It was a whisper. A black pool stained the pillow under the man's head. Annie was gone.

A familiar fear, too tired to rise, gave way to trembling rage as she turned away. Sheila cried for the man who died offering her the protection of his house and prayed for the man she still loved.

Chapter 16
Southern Italy
Ciro Michi's Estate
Saturday, March 13

"Leave me alone," Michi commanded. His children shuffled from the room. He leaned forward, eyes glued to the screen. Pino Pinzini shifted uncomfortably next to him.

The BBC reported from their London Office.

"The world is in shock today at the still ongoing disaster in the nations of South Central Africa. Initial reports indicate massive structural failure of the Kariba Dam. The few reports we now have suggest the dam has disintegrated. This failure precipitated cataclysmic flooding in the downstream regions and, it appears, the Cahora Bassa Dam also failed when waters from Kariba overran the Cahora Bassa Lake. Though accurate reports are short supply, satellite imagery suggests there will be widespread damage and significant loss of life. We will keep you abreast of developments throughout the evening.

"In other news from the region, according to a statement just received from Zambia's Ministry of the Interior, Cedric Mwanyisa, longtime President of Zimbabwe has been shot in an apparent assassination attempt. The President is en route to South Africa where he will be treated for his injuries. The Zambian Ministry reports Mwanyisa has been stabilized but remains in critical condition. The President of Zimbabwe was in Zambia attending a convention of heads of states for members of the Southern African Development Community.

"It is indeed a dark day for Africa. Our thoughts and prayers are with—"

Michi switched off the television and turned to his guest.

Pinzini settled back in his chair and rubbed his face, trying to figure out what had happened. Removing Kariba Dam seemed simple enough. Pinzini already had the Zimbabwean President's signature awarding his firm the contract for the reconstruction. It was a contract worth four billion US dollars. But if the Zimbabwean President was dead, the post-dated signature would be useless.

Michi's cold eyes stared at the fat man in front of him. "I thought you came here to tell me everything was in order?"

"Esposito phoned to tell me it was only a matter of time," Pinzini replied. "How could we have known of the assassination attempt?"

"Yes. You are in an unfortunate position." Michi's words dropped like stones. "I suggest you pray this president lives."

Chapter 17
Mazabuka, Zambia
Saturday March 13
Early Morning

The Cessna Skymaster touched down on the dirt runway just outside of Mazabuka, Zambia and bounced to a stop near a hanger of rusting corrugated iron. Joey "The Rat" Greer killed the engines and pulled the key.

The twin propellers left an empty silence. The Rat popped open the side door and re-lit an old cigar, squinting as smoke burned his eyes. "I hear someone tried to bag a big elephant up north," he said.

"That so?" Aaron tried to sound casual. "Did they get him, then?"

Greer puckered his lips around the fat stump in his mouth. "Don't know yet. Last I heard, they were still tracking it, waiting to see if the old beast would fall down."

"That is a shame," Aaron replied. "When I hunt, I always like a nice clean kill. Keeps things from getting messy."

"True that." The Rat said. "Still, sometimes I think there's some kind of juju that keeps the old going longer than they should, you know?" He chuckled. A soft, unhappy snort.

"Damn shame," Aaron replied.

"Ya. But you know what they say. The smell of blood sometimes brings out all kinds of hungries. The lions and hyenas will probably find him now."

Aaron stared out into the night from his seat beside their pilot. The failure hung heavy over them. Stuart and Daniel slipped into a deep brooding silence soon after they had met up at their rendezvous point. The adrenaline rush had fallen away and left them alone with their grief.

"I hope so," Aaron whispered.

Chapter 18
Lusaka, Zambia
Saturday, March 13

Power outages were common enough in the capitol, but it seemed this one had come to stay. Though few Zambians relative to the overall population lived with electricity at home, the infrastructure of the country had grown increasingly dependent on Kariba as a primary energy source. Internet cafés, ATM machines and cell phones had become the norm for Zambia's new generation of city dwellers. Water stopped flowing. Pumps stood idle next to waiting vehicles.

The country held its breath for information.

Zambian news and television agencies went black. The BBC broadcasts via shortwave radio provided the only news from a very dark continent. Here and there the fortunate few huddled around battery powered shortwave radios waiting for England to bring them news of their own country. ShopRite and Game, Lusaka's upscale grocer and merchandise, had already sold out all batteries. These sold on a cash-only basis by enterprising managers who set up kiosks on the sidewalk where there was enough light to see.

The concomitant shock sobered the country. The few shops with natural light stayed open, working on a cash basis, but there were few shoppers. The country reeled as the import of the news began to sink in.

Within hours, churches filled with people praying for rescue efforts, and airports filled with others trying to get out. The combination of the assassination attempt and the Kariba disaster did not bode well for expatriates whose perspective of Africa had been shaped by stories of Rwanda genocide.

Military police patrolled major commercial interests of the country, hoping to stave off the rising threat of riots and opportunistic robberies.

Chapter 19
Lusaka, Zambia
Saturday, March 13

Auxiliary generators hummed outside Lusaka International Airport to supply electricity necessary to power computers and satellite uplinks. Terminal tanker trucks fueled planes waiting for departure. Most inbound traffic diverted to Nairobi.

The British Airways attendant recognized Sheila's fragile state. She assumed Sheila lost someone in the flood and upgraded her to first class. Sheila didn't care if the accommodation reflected her red-lined eyes or their desire to keep an eye on her.

She stuffed the ticket in her handbag and thanked the attendant before going upstairs. Sheila scanned faces for the man with the sickle scar above his nose before slipping into the ladies room. He had not followed her here.

The bathroom reeked of urine and worse. She turned the tap. A thread of water drooled over a copper stain in the enamel sink. The airport's generators couldn't help it if the city's water pumps went off line. Sheila leaned over the sink and squinted at puffy bags under her eyes. She couldn't decide if she were tired or hungry, afraid for her life, or scared to death about Daniel and her father. There was no way she could find Daniel now. He knew she was planning to stay with her grandparents in the United Kingdom. If she didn't get there, he wouldn't know where to find her.

The call came for her flight. She left the drooling tap and moved directly through airport security.

Sheila carefully gave a wide berth to people repeating what little they knew of the country's news. The Kariba disaster filled every conversation. She unsuccessfully tried to connect it with what she knew Daniel and her father were doing. Daniel would know where to find her. She couldn't call him, couldn't find her phone. Besides, the country's entire communication network floundered in a tangle of widespread power outages and no cell signal. Everyone wanted to call someone. She would have to wait until she got to London. Sheila boarded the plane with nothing but her handbag. Her suitcase still lay on her bed in the house with Annie's dead husband.

British Airway's flight 4775 taxied while the staff mindlessly performed the preflight emergency presentation. The Boeing 747 turned at the base of the runway for takeoff. Africa sped past the window. Tears blurred the green landscape. The jet lifted off with a bump. Sheila leaned back in her seat and closed her eyes.

Chapter 20
Lusaka, Zambia
Saturday, March 13

Lusaka went dark. Usually, power failures impacted specific areas. But this darkness felt uncanny, even in Africa.

Street kids began to move out. They already knew their targets. Enough time on the street and one began to notice things. People came and went. Street kids saw everything. They knew which houses stood empty. Faces were easy to track when one had nothing else to do. White faces were even easier.

Simon watched his gang swarm the wall like rats. Most of the boys had not yet reached their twelfth year, but life on the street made them hard, wiry and high. Simon carried a bottle of glue in his pocket mixed with a little gasoline. He pulled up the cap, inhaled noisily and squeezed the fumes into his nose. Simon made his living on gasoline and glue—a little something to take the edge off the emptiness and hunger. Because he had money, he had followers. Followers hungry enough to stay desperate. Hunger was a powerful motivator.

They gathered around him, white eyes glowing. Simon put the glue back into his pocket, and shook his head at a nine year old who begged for a hit. Their deteriorated clothes showed various shades of dun and rag in the dark.

Simon led the way and hung from the security bars bolted around the front window. Taking a garden stone, he reached through the bars and smashed the glass, sweeping remaining shards from the metal frame. Two of the larger boys clambered up on the raised planter in front of the window and pushed against the iron bars. They rocked back and forth against the white bars until a bolt came loose from the block wall, then prized the barrier away from the window enough to squeeze past. The others followed, stepping on broken glass.

Bloody footprints tramped across tiled floors.

The house belonged to two single women who worked at the Lusaka International School. The school offered an International Baccalaureate, catering to wealthy Zambians and children of expatriates. The street boys knew nothing of international certificates, but they saw the kind of cars the teachers drove and knew where each teacher's car parked at night. The school was their beat. Their block. Simon made sure of that.

None of Simon's boys went to school. Instead, they found entertainment where they could. With glue. Or with each other. Occasionally, they would sneak into another gang's area and 'borrow' a girl. Sometimes the girl would stay for a while, but usually she would leave.

It was easier for girls to find steady employment.

The teachers had left. Their gardener said they'd gone to the airport because of the trouble. Simon didn't know what that meant. But he did know tonight would be different. Tonight meant food. Real food.

The boys found the kitchen first. They fought over the seven boxes of long-life milk in the fridge. Simon squatted in the center of the kitchen table and watched. The conflict grew to a fistfight, which stopped when an older boy smashed the youngest across his face. The little one fell back, cracked his head on the counter, and lay still. The rest ignored him, stepping on him to climb on the counter so they could raid higher cupboards. Simon would be the last to eat. Even with street children, a few of the customs of hospitality remained. He pulled the glue from his pocket again and took another hit, pushing back the hungry pain in his stomach. In exchange for hospitality, and protection, they did anything he wanted. The boys ate everything they could find. One tore open a paper bag of sugar and sat in the corner scooping it into his mouth. There were no smiles. No voices.

The boys settled in the kitchen, surrounded by the debris of their feeding frenzy. Sugar Boy eventually fell into some kind of convulsion, and though the others glanced in his direction, they left him alone. Simon climbed down from the table and took the sugar packet from the boy's twitching hands. He poured the last handful into his palm, poked at it with the tip of his tongue and walked through the house.

Bureau drawers stood open in the bedroom. School papers lay scattered on the floor. The teachers had left in a hurry. Most of their clothes still hung in the closet. Simon found the bathroom and opened the vanity, hands feeling the contents. Pads, tampons, tooth brushes, razor blades. Listerine. He licked the last of the sugar from his palm, sipped at the Listerine and sucked toothpaste from the tube.

He would stay here a while. The teachers probably wouldn't be back right away. If he could keep the boys inside during the daylight hours, they could take their time and leave the following night.

Simon walked back to the bedroom. He could smell them. The women's fragrance lingered. He flopped an armful of clothing on the bed and climbed in, clinging to the mass, breathing in the clean smell.

Simon's thumb found his mouth, and he fell asleep.

Chapter 21
Heathrow, England
Sunday, March 14
Early Morning

Her plane landed early Sunday morning after exhaustion and the complimentary wine forced sleep on Sheila. The long hours of thinking had been intolerable. She forced herself through the customs counter, giving the address of her grandparents in the Downs as her destination. She didn't know what she would do once she got there. Her mind felt numb. Too tired to think.

"Sorry to hear about what happened in Africa." The custom's officer shook her head. "It is just horrible."

Sheila could only nod and watch the officer press the stamp into the green passport.

"Welcome to the United Kingdom."

Sheila moved into the terminal mall. Its opulence clean and surreal against the gritty indifference to dirt in the developing world. Had she felt more alive, she might have felt self-conscious, out of fashion. But she didn't care. Her whole body ached.

Sheila walked into a kiosk and paid for a copy of the London Times.

"Your receipt, madam." The attendant interrupted her.

Sheila took the paper to a table in a café, ordered strong black coffee and sat down to read. Photographs of the lower Zambezi filled the front page. Casualty estimates kept climbing. Some said millions. For once, African news permeated headlines.

There were pictures, too, of refugee camps for those who lived in the regulated flood zones. Photos taken before the dam gave way. A red arrow superimposed on the aerial photograph showed where the camp had been. Not a single trace remained. Water dominated the pictures. Dotted black lines indicated where the river normally ran. Red highlighted areas showing population centers now underwater. She read on, wiping the tears off the newsprint.

The counter called her coffee order. Sheila didn't notice.

At the bottom of the front page, she saw a report about an assassination attempt on Mwanyisa. Suddenly a line blurred; she felt dizzy. The article quoted a statement received early on Friday before Zambia's communications networks went off-line.

According to Zambia's Press Secretary, elite military teams pursued the assailants and intercepted them on the outskirts of Lusaka. The terrorists opened fire but were subsequently killed in the ensuing fight. In order to preserve the integrity of their investigation, Zambian officials can release no further details at this time.

Sheila snatched the paper from the table, tried to read it again, but the words blurred. She stood, shoving the chair away from her into another customer. It couldn't be true. She gasped for breath and stumbled from the cafe, aware only of the need to get away from the newspaper, the horror, the loss, and thoughts of Daniel and her father lying dead somewhere in Africa.

The terminal spun. She moved past the duty free shop, dizzied by the mirrors. Travelers and shoppers eyed her suspiciously and moved out of her way as she crashed through a set of double glass doors into a confectionary with delicate bonbons and Swiss Chocolates stacked in neat pyramids.

Sheila gripped the counter for balance; stared at the cashier. "Where is my mother?"

"I'm sorry? Was she just here?" he asked, wiping hands on his apron.

A policeman, alerted by the public followed her into the shop. "Madam. May I help you?"

"No. I'm trying to find mother. I'm trying to get away from him." Her words became incoherent. Sheila pushed roughly past the policeman. "Sorry," she mumbled, "but I have to get out of here. I have to get to mother. She has to know about this." Sheila stumbled and landed against a revolving rack of coffee mugs that read *I love London* knocking several onto the floor.

"Madam, I must ask you to step outside." The policeman followed the crazed woman further back into the shop.

He found Sheila lying wedged where she had collapsed in a fetal position between a greeting card stand and a keychain display. The woman's hair was tangled and her sandals and attire hardly suited to the chill English weather. In her right hand the woman held a crumpled page of what appeared to be The Times of London. Newspaper ink stained her reddened face.

He took her vitals and radioed for help.

"Stay back, please." He spoke to crowding pedestrians. "The woman is obviously in distress."

The shopkeeper dragged displays out of the way so the terminal emergency crews could attend to her. Gentle hands moved Sheila to a stretcher and tucked a clean white sheet around her.

The guard found Sheila's passport. "The emergency contact information is in Zimbabwe. I'll run this passport through security and see if we can get a local address."

Two other medics wheeled her from the crowded shop. The attending nurse spoke into the mouthpiece of the radio hanging from his epaulette, requesting emergency transportation to the hospital.

Other security arrived, opening a way through the gathered people. The emergency staff wheeled the stretcher out of the store while someone fitted a blood pressure cuff.

Chapter 22
Ashbury, England
Sunday, March 14

The telephone rang in an empty hallway. A clatter in the kitchen followed. A round woman marched down the narrow hall, wiping her hands on a dishtowel. "I'm coming. I'm coming."

Plump fingers plucked the phone from its cradle and listened.

"Yes, I am Mavis Pickering." She squinted at a hole in the plaster wall, trying to hear. It was getting harder these days.

"My goodness gracious. I didn't know she was to be in the country. This is quite a shock." She squinted again, listening.

"Of course," she replied. "I just have to get the gingerbread out of the oven, then we'll be right down. Might take me a bit to find my husband. He's off tromping around outside." She turned toward the door, "Oh my goodness. It might take us a bit to get there in the old car, but tell her we'll be down just the same."

She replaced the cradle and hurried back to the kitchen.

"Just as well I've made some gingerbread, now, isn't it." She said to no one. "Seems as though we are going to have some company." The kitchen window overlooked a garden that butted up against the green hills. "Now, where is Cyril?"

She heard the front door open and turned to rush back down the hallway.

"Cyril! Thank God you're back!"

The man stopped mid-hum. "I've only been out to the post box." His frame was as spare as hers was not, and his wellies flopped around at the tops. He pulled off his tweed and stepped easily from his boots while mumbling about a nagging woman.

"Why were you at the post box? It is Sunday, Cyril. You know there is no post on Sunday."

"Of course, I know there is no post on Sunday, dearest." He spoke with long practiced patience.

"Then why did you go to the post box?"

"Because, dearest, I was putting a letter *in* the post."

"You shouldn't have left." Her words tumbled. "The London police called. Sheila and the baby are in the hospital. We must go and pick them up!" She lifted his jacket from the coat hanger and thrust it back toward him.

"Sheila? Sheila who? We don't know any Sheila with a baby. The police? What are you talking about?"

Mavis huffed. "Of course we do, you old stick, our Sheila is in the hospital."

"What?" Cyril began stuffing his arms into the jacket.

"Sheila Hall Smith," she persisted, "you know, Kathy's girl. Have you forgotten?" She talked while she fumbled her coat over her apron.

"Of course not, but since when did she have a baby? We were just in Zimbabwe at their wedding," he said.

"Well, I don't know, but the police said she was taken to the hospital from the airport. Where have you put the keys, Cyril?" She pawed under the newspaper. "Seems they found her in the airport, having a bit of a rough time. So they carried her off to the hospital where she is now. I'm afraid something might be terribly wrong."

"Is she alone then? What about that new husband of hers?" he asked.

"Who's to know? The man on the phone said doctors were concerned she might have experienced some kind of shock. Hurry up, then." Mavis moved to the front door.

"A baby? We didn't hear from her before now. I wonder if she's tried to email us?"

"Don't know," she said. "We really should get Bobby to come over and tell us why the computer isn't working. I always did like the post better. Far more reliable."

Cyril opened a drawer and retrieved the car keys. "Did you turn off the oven then?"

"Oh, my goodness!" She bustled back to the kitchen while her husband fetched a decent pair of shoes.

Then they stepped outside into the crisp air of the Downs.

Chapter 23
Madagascar
Sunday, March 14

The man woke slowly, pushed up by degrees through the fog of unconsciousness. Absolute darkness and stifling heat pressed around him with the same intensity as his raging thirst. He reached up to touch his eyes, checked to see if they were indeed open. He tried to remember, but heat and thirst kept interrupting. In his mind, he saw a single blinking light. A red one. That was all.

Thoughts scattered like beads fallen from a broken string. His mind groped around, but wherever he turned there was only the single blinking light.

Perhaps I am dead, he thought. He hadn't expected to be so thirsty when he died.

He flung his arm to feel the sides of his coffin, but instead his hand fell on warm steel. After some consideration, he sat up carefully. His head ached with the effort, he could not swallow. This must be hell, he determined. He had always figured he was going the other direction. He didn't care.

He needed a drink.

He rolled to his knees and pushed himself onto his feet. With hands outstretched he rose to his full height and cracked his head on unforgiving steel. Tiny sparks swam around him, but he kept his legs.

With one arm over his head, he began to move. He still felt no panic in the close darkness. Most people, he thought, would panic in this kind of a place. I am only thirsty. Hundreds of pipes blocked his path and threatened to twist his ankles, but he pushed on.

He felt his way down a kind of iron alley, smashing shins on sharp edges, stepping over obstacles in his path. The air held a growing unpleasant smell. He stopped before a barricade, swept hands over it. It felt familiar, but still he could not remember. It was just too dark. He felt as if he was swimming and couldn't remember which way was up.

An obstacle tangled his feet and he fell against it. An odd tingle pricked his scalp before he recognized what it was. He rolled himself off the dead body, gagging in the smell of death, and lay beside it on the uneven, cluttered surface.

Then it occurred to him. If he is dead, then I am not.

Again he pushed himself off the ground, groping until he found a tilted staircase with an iron railing. He knew the way. Knowledge without memory. His body moved up the slanting stairs with a familiar confidence. At the top, his hands found an iron wheel and turned it.

Instinctively, he pushed his shoulder against the hatch.

Light and fresh air exploded around him, pushing back the reek. He staggered, shielding eyes against the brilliance. His head throbbed anew, but the air felt delicious and sweet and clean.

He pulled himself from the after-hatch and crawled onto the deck of the submarine. The iron hulk listed hard to port and nested among the trees. Weeds and debris of all kinds clung to its side as if someone had attempted to decorate the hull for a party.

The front left diving plane had been sheared off completely and lay not far away. He stared. Grey iron under the hot sun burned his hands and elbows, but after the smoldering stench in the hold, the air felt cool and fresh and pure. He stood, steadied himself and walked toward the cigarette deck at the rear of the bridge. The air sucked the sweat and stink from his clothing. Number 2 periscope stood unharmed like a single digit raised in defiance of the wreckage around it. The other periscope looked like the broken leg of a stick insect, oddly twisted and useless.

The man turned and saw, almost half a mile beyond the stern planes, a beach. Beyond that the turbid ocean spread out of sight through a tropic haze.

He closed his eyes. Think. Again, the blinking red light. Emergency lighting. Emergency. Something had happened. Something he could not, or would not remember.

A voice brought him back. A brown boy stood staring up at him. The man nodded a greeting, unable to understand. The child reached into a plastic bag and withdrew a mango.

He held it up for the man who tried to drive his submarine into the forest.

Chapter 24
Johannesburg, South Africa
Sunday, March 14

According to plan, Daniel, Stuart and Aaron left the country as soon as they could after the operation. Kathy had traveled ahead to South Africa a few days before. She wanted to know everything about their plan, but Stuart was vague. He had told her to fly to South Africa, ignore the papers, lay low, he would meet her there.

Stuart didn't know how to tell Kathy. How does a man tell his wife their daughter is dead? How could explain the guilt that threatened to drown out every other conscious thought?

When she saw him, she knew. They held each other for a long time in the hotel room.

Outside, Africa reeled under the aftereffects of the Kariba disaster. Inside, private grief overwhelmed them. Light faded from the room. Waves of sadness swept over them. A cloud threatening never to lift.

The rage of memories invaded Stuart's dreams. Sheila played in the sandbox they built for her off the veranda. He heard the rattle of her little voice talking to her dolly about tea, or the venison they were going to have when the men got back from hunting. The voice haunted him and the feel of her little fingers woke him at night. Thunder howled and he would see her standing beside their bed, knocking politely on the mosquito net. 'I think Dolly would feel safer in your bed.' She climbed in with her doll and squeeze in between them, ignoring the hot. Little fingers would fiddle with his beard until she fell asleep. Then he would wake up to lift her from the bed and carry her back to her own room, except Sheila wasn't there.

He and Kathy were alone. Alone in this terrible new future.

Sheila was gone.

Stuart got out of bed, stood on the balcony of their room. The lights of Johannesburg blinked back at him. He remembered the day Enoch Mpundu first interfered in their life. If only he had watched over her more carefully. If only.

In the morning, Stuart and Kathy sat at the table in their room, sipping complimentary coffee, more tired than the night before.

"We need to contact my parents," she said. "They can notify the rest of the family."

"You want to call them?" Stuart asked.

"No. I'm afraid they might not take it well." Kathy looked out their second story window at the streets of Johannesburg. Pedestrians moved about, oblivious to their nightmare. "I think I need to tell them in person."

"Yes. That's probably best. I'll have to stay here, of course, in case I'm needed to tie up loose ends." He didn't have to explain.

Kathy reached across the table and covered his hand with her own. "Will you manage okay by yourself?"

"I'll manage." Stuart cleared his throat. "I think I'll volunteer at the British Embassy. They could use my help coordinating relief efforts. Might find it handy to have someone who speaks Shona. It will keep me busy. You can leave tomorrow. I'll make the arrangements."

"Stuart." She waited for his eyes. "This wasn't your fault."

Chapter 25
The Flood Zone
Monday, March 15

Daniel Smith stood in the mud by a tangle of debris. Above him, a man hung incongruously among the labyrinth of power cables and tree limbs. He would have to be gotten down. Vultures slouched in the upper branches of the snarl, just a few feet away from the dangling man. The smell kept them close, but they were full.

Food was everywhere in the flats.

Daniel had worked feverishly over the past thirty hours. After dropping Stuart and Aaron in Johannesburg, The Rat flew Daniel into the Kariba wash zone. If he stood still, memories engulfed him. He couldn't let them come. Wouldn't. He didn't know what he might do.

"Carlton, toss me a line. I'm going to climb up after him." Daniel called to the man who stood behind him on a sort of bank.

Daniel and Carlton met at the temporary Red Cross Emergency relief camp the day before. Daniel checked in with the camp director who happened to be a German doctor. She insisted he just call her Gretta. She looked suspiciously at Daniel, but few Red Cross volunteers had arrived and already there was too much to do.

Daniel filled out the paperwork as Stanley Heath in case some kind of an investigation opened up over the shooting. But he didn't much care. He almost wished someone would come after him and put him out of his misery. He felt like a wounded buffalo, bristling mad from pain, just waiting for someone to cross him out. When Carlton showed up at the relief camp, the two set out as a team. They were well matched physically and bonded under the shadow of tragedy.

"I don't think you'd better, Stan. It doesn't look stable," Carlton looked up at the mess of twisted debris.

"Just throw me the damn line. I'm going up," Daniel said.

Each volunteer team worked a specific area coordinated via a sat link from Cape Town. Every team carried short range walkie talkies and a GPS. Previous landmarks didn't exist. On the flight in, Daniel had seen, here and there, the bare rock underbelly of the Zambezi flood plain staring up at him. Like some perverted monster, the flood stripped the land and the bedrock mirrored back the sun.

Daniel tied the rope around his middle and picked his way into the jumbled mess towering almost forty feet above him.

Mud sucked at his feet and insects swarmed his arms and neck. He pulled himself up by an electric cable. The bugs feasted, but he clenched his jaw and welcomed the pain. Focus. Keep working. Don't think.

A wire wrapped branch suspended horizontally above him. A death trap or a bridge, he didn't care. Scrambling up, he walked across the bridge toward the body. It hung wedged in the crotch of a tree, pressed in by the roiling flood. It must have been a horrible way to die.

The rope about his waist snagged and Daniel pulled hard to free it. He ignored the black-eyed stare of the hunched buzzards and stepped into the tree beneath the man. Impossibly, the man opened his eyes. A flutter of sound. "Mezi." Water.

"Carlton," Daniel shouted. "He's alive. Get him some water." He couldn't believe it. Crossing branches pinned the man's arm behind him, an effective, macabre prison.

Carlton tossed up a line with a bottle of water tied to the other end. The man stared blankly at Daniel, barely conscious.

"Mezi," Daniel said. His voice was tender now. "Open your mouth."

Carefully, Daniel poured in the water. Slowly. Drop by drop. Not too much at one time. Daniel didn't realize he was crying.

They found seven dead today. Four living. Three of them died soon after being found. The human spirit hung on until help was at hand. Then, when they relaxed, they died. Only one child lived through the ordeal of rescue. A little girl, about twelve, though it was hard to tell her age. The water completely stripped her clothing. When she regained consciousness, Daniel pulled off his own shirt to make a sort of tunic. They took the girl back to camp and put her in the care of Gretta.

#

Carlton owned a farm in Zambia's central province. When the news reached him, he had hopped on his motorbike and traveled all the way to the flood zone. He was a decent sort and gave Daniel space. He knew Daniel needed to work this disaster in order to stave off one of his own. He made space for Daniel's bursts of grief and rage. Carlton was steady, methodical and passionate.

"I've radioed base. Let them know we have another coming," Carlton said. The steady influx of water revived the trapped man considerably, but pain ground away at his consciousness and several times they thought they'd lost him. Once, Daniel braced his own back against an opposing branch, so he could administer chest compressions to the man who was then, still, almost vertical.

At last, after several frustrating hours, they managed to free and lower the wounded man to the ground. The grotesque arm looked like it would have to be amputated. Carlton fixed a tourniquet. They lifted him onto the army stretcher and began the long walk back to base.

Chapter 26
New York Stock Exchange
New York, NY
Monday, March 15

Traders pressed together in clusters across the exchange amid the usual chaos and frenetic energy. Bids and cell phones rang out across the paper littered floor. Today, copper was gold.

Investors either rode above the swells of national disasters or were crushed beneath them. With the loss of their primary power supply, Zambia's copper mines floundered. Zambian Copper plummeted. South American copper soared. Supply and demand.

Travis Sander's phone rang. It was the Italian. He had set up a foreign brokerage account and willingly paid the commission. For the last month, the man purchased as much copper as Travis could buy. The Italian had been specific. *Only* South American copper. Cerro Verde, Peru. El Abra, Candelaria, and Ojos Del Salado, Chile. The company operating those mines planned a grand expansion. They needed capital. Shares were cheap.

Travis took the call. "Yes?" The New York Stock Exchange didn't believe in pleasantries.

"Sell my shares in Pinzini & Blaise," the Italian said.

"How many?" Travis asked.

"All of them." Then the Italian hung up.

Travis had to look up the ticker symbol. Pinzini and Blaise, an Italian-based civil engineering firm, wasn't listed on the NYSE. It was on the pink sheets. Ticker symbol PIBL.PK. Apparently the company didn't want to open their books to the Securities and Exchange Commission. Travis initiated the sell-off before he left the chaos for lunch. A thought teased its way into his brain. Something about the Italian didn't add up.

Travis figured a hot dog from a street vender was healthier than a day on Wall Street with no break.

He stepped out onto the cold New York sidewalk and pulled his coat shut. The city endured another late snow. What hadn't been trucked out of the city, crowded in dirty piles in every available space. Vinny competed with the piles and managed to keep selling oversized, overpriced food to people who truly appreciated a good hot dog.

"Hey, Vinny." Travis pulled a tenner from his wallet and slid it under the napkin dispenser. "Give me the works."

"Livin' on the edge, eh?" Vinny stuffed a dog into a cold bun and gave it the treatment.

"Thanks." Travis grabbed the dog and his change and headed across the cobbled street to find a place out of the wind. He backed up against the JP Morgan placard and shoved the sandwich into his mouth.

Then it hit him. The Italian's stock holdings. The news. A destroyed hydroelectric dam meant no power. No power meant no copper. Zambian copper mines were effectively shut down until some other power solution had been found, and the Italian's South American stocks tripled in value. The Italian knew something. He was the man holding all the aces. No one trusts investments that big to dumb luck. The connection with the disaster in Africa left Travis shaken and feeling dirty. He wasn't exactly sure what Pinzini and Blaise had to do with it all.

Travis needed another line of work. The NYSE was messy business. The pressure already ruined his attempts at married life. It wasn't worth it.

He wiped his mouth, tossed the rest of his hotdog and dialed Zachary Morgan of the New York Times.

"Zach, Travis Sander here. I think you might want to buy me supper."

Chapter 27
New York City
Tuesday, March 16

Wind whipped down the frozen streets. Vinny turned off his lights and studied the apartment building from his car. His hands thawed over the warm air vents.

Vinny knew most of the brokers who figured as people of interest to his boss, but this was different. This man was a customer. The rest didn't buy Vinny's food, and Vinny didn't want to kill him. Someone from the Old Country ordered a hit. Someone who still pulled weight in the Big Apple. Vinny shrugged. Not his problem. Find the guy; take him out; make it quick. No sense crossing the wrong people over a little sentimentality. He turned up the heat. Vinny hated winter. Hell would be an upgrade.

A taxi pulled up to the apartment. Vinny leaned forward and gripped the wheel. Travis Sander emerged, pulled up his coat collar and started down the steps to the taxi.

Vinny fingered the pistol in his lap. I hate my job, he thought. I stand out in all kinds of weather, watching faces, killing people slowly with hot dogs and spend my nights following men around. Some life.

Vinny tailed the taxi, giving it space. He didn't know where the man was going, just that it needed to happen tonight. Vinny let two cars fill in between them. Travis was probably just going for a little nightlife.

Wouldn't that be nice, Vinny thought.

His engine lurched and he glanced at the dash. The temperature needle pressed hard against the pin. It lurched again and white steam crowded from the hood.

Vinny cursed, and pulled over. He fumed with the vehicle for a few minutes before he grabbed his coat, and hit the sidewalk, going back the way he came.

Chapter 28
Paddy Reilly's Bar
Murray Hill, New York, New York
Tuesday Evening, March 16

Zachary Morgan paid the cover charge.

"These guys are good." He nodded toward a band. "Heard 'em last time I was here. Order me a Guinness," Zachary said. "I'm going to the 'toolshed'."

Travis Sander ordered two beers at the bar and found a booth away from the band. He took a long sip and wiped foam from his lip. He slouched in his favorite pair of jeans and a Notre Dame sweatshirt. He'd actually attended university in Pennsylvania before joining the crazies at the New York Stock Exchange. The sweatshirt came from his wife's brother. Ex-wife, now.

Travis took another drink and Zachary returned from the bathroom.

His friend pulled the beer up close. "Now, that's a thing of beauty." He fished a notepad from his pocket. "What have you got?"

"Probably enough to get me killed, but not enough to get me fired," Travis said.

"Sounds like a story."

"Here's the deal. The information I'm about to give you—"

"I know. I know." Zachary held up his hand. "I can't tell anyone where I got it, I have to make my own connection to the crime, and I never spoke with you in my life."

"Something like that." Travis smiled.

"Do you know how complicated that makes my life?" Zachary asked.

"Hey, a complicated life is better than no life. If my guy is tied into what I suspect, a man's life doesn't mean much to him. If it's okay with you, I'd like to keep mine intact."

"You sound serious." Zachary studied his friend. "You doin' okay?"

Travis turned toward the band. A couple of old men were making an embarrassing attempt at dance.

"I'm getting out," Travis said, finally. "I'm one of the only men on the floor that takes a lunch break. If a guy believes a hot dog is healthier than his job, he's pretty far gone."

Zachary chuckled. "You have a point there, but everyone eats hot dogs. Hell, this is America. We eat hot dogs and do penance when we get old by becoming a vegetarian or getting diabetes or cancer and then we send the bills to our insurance provider. Either way we grow old and fat."

"Vinny says hot dogs are the secret to a long life," Travis said.

"How so?"

"Preservatives. Claims they'll make you last forever. Embalm you before you're dead."

"Great. America's secret to immortality. Who needs the fountain of youth?" Zachary painted headlines in the air. "Eat Hot Dogs: Live Long and Prosper. I'm starting to like this Vinny. Who is he?"

"Just a street vendor who is likely going to live much longer than I am because his idea of a stressful day is having four people in his hotdog line at the same time."

71

"You're serious about quitting, aren't you?" Zachary looked hard at his friend. "Is this about Lisa?"

"Maybe a little." Travis paused as the waiter stopped by with more beer.

"It was a beautiful wedding. She was a hottie. I figured you'd be able to settle down with her." Zachary winked.

"You're not helping." Travis made a face.

"You're right. I'm sorry. I know it sounds trite, but people like me— we want the storybook ending. Want things to work out, you know? I guess I thought you had a chance. Wanted you to have a chance."

"Me too."

"What is she doing, anyway?" Zachary asked.

"Who? Lisa?" Travis diverted.

"No, Mother Theresa."

"Fine. She's back in Pennsylvania. Working at a bank."

"You ever see her?"

"No. Can we talk about something else?"

"Sure." Zachary let it drop. "Tell me about your find."

"Okay. You know the dam that broke last Friday?"

Zachary nodded.

"As soon as trading opened Monday, copper shares started to climb."

"Connect the dots," Zachary said.

"Zambia is—or was—responsible for a large percentage of the world's copper supply. Zambia's mines, maybe Zimbabwe's, too—I don't know if they do copper as well—were powered by electricity from the dam. According to the little bit of research I did, the dam was built for that purpose."

"What purpose?" Zachary interrupted.

"To power the mines. Of course, it was presented to the world as this wonderful bit of western generosity for the 'poor unfortunates' of central Africa, but it was only about money. Lots of it. The hydro project enabled mines to extract copper at maximum profit—little of which actually made its way to the African people."

"Sounds like business as usual." Zachary jotted a few notes. "Keeping up so far."

"Anyway, when the dam disappeared, almost half the world's copper supply went off line. Zambia can still get copper out of the ground. There is some other power available, but it is expensive and will price them out of the market."

"So where is the story?"

"I'm almost there." Travis finished his beer. "About one month ago, I get this call from some guy in Italy who asks me to buy up all the copper shares I can get my hands on."

"Now the guy is pissed because they aren't worth anything?" Zachary asked. "Sounds like Wall Street."

"No." Travis lowered his voice. "The man's shares have almost tripled in value."

"How do you figure?"

"He only wanted stock in South American mines."

"No shit." Zachary's pen stopped. He looked up. "What kind of investment are we talking about?"

"Somewhere in the neighborhood of 300 million dollars. Maybe more."

"What the Fu—!" Zachary spoke into a lull in the music. Heads turned. He lowered his voice. "Where does a guy come up with that kind of liquid cash in a month?"

"Legally, you mean?" Travis matched his friend's volume. "I don't think you do."

Travis leaned in across the table. "Either this guy has a crystal ball, or he got a tip off that a certain number of mines would be knocked off line because of a certain 'natural disaster.'"

Zachary shook his head. "How does some guy know when a natural disaster is going to come?"

"That is the question."

Travis let it sink in. The media had been dominated by news of search and recovery efforts underway and the mounting humanitarian effort for the affected nations. The humanitarian crisis was just a red herring. The real story was in the mines.

"If this is true, it means this whole dam thing wasn't a *natural* disaster." Zachary leaned on the word natural. "The estimated death toll is over five million."

Travis didn't reply.

"Unless I can name my source," Zachary said, "my editor will never go with this. It is too big. A guy can't just waltz in and claim the world's single largest natural disaster to date is the work of some bad guy who already has too much cash. Unless I have proof, I've got no story."

Travis shook his head. "Remember, I don't want to become a number in this natural disaster."

"You're kidding me, right? You tease me with what is the biggest story ever, and yet you don't give me a single solid string to follow?"

"That all you care about? Your big break?" Travis retorted.

"Yes and no. I could use a break. Who couldn't? The big deal is that the pond scum who did this needs to be brought to justice."

"I'm glad to see there's a spark of decency in you," Travis replied. "There is more."

"I'm listening."

"About a month ago, this same guy also purchased a controlling interest in Pinzini & Blaise, an Italian based, civil engineering firm."

"What kind of civil engineering firm?" Zachary scrawled the names on his pad.

"Dams," Travis replied. "Big ones. Aswan. Hoover. You get the idea. He wants to sell those shares. All of them."

Zachary looked confused again. "Help me."

"Okay. Investors haven't woken up to the fact that someone is going to have to put that dam back into place. The average mom and pop investors just watch the news and call in to make their purchases. Serious investors know better."

"So why would he sell out? That doesn't make sense. If he wanted to sell out, he should have waited until investors got wind of the idea and prices spiked."

"Now you're tracking. It doesn't make sense."

"Give me a scenario," Zachary said.

"He must have thought they were going to get a valuable contract. Then things changed."

"That's impossible. Too many leaps of faith. How would he have known they might get the contract? Except to have a signed deal with a decision maker before the dam was destroyed..."

"Right." Travis waited for his friend to catch up.

Realization spread across Zachary's face. He whispered, "Mwanyisa."

"Precisely. Maybe Pinzini & Blaise had a contract in hand, but then a key signature went and got himself shot."

"What's this guy's name?" Zachary asked.

"Ciro Michi."

Zachary pushed his beer away and rubbed his face. "I've got some serious work to do." He shook his head and stood up from the table. He felt numb, unsure where to start.

"I guess all you have to do, as the old adage says, is 'follow the money.'" Travis said.

"This is huge. I've got to go." Zachary Morgan grabbed his notepad and walked out.

Travis watched him leave. "Thanks for buying," he mumbled.

Chapter 29
Johannesburg, South Africa
March 16

Stuart put Kathy on the plane that morning. It had been difficult to say goodbye, but she planned to be gone only a few days and would return as soon as it felt right to leave her parents.

Traffic crawled out of Johannesburg, and Stuart arrived at the British High Commission in Pretoria almost two hours later.

Stuart presented his British passport which he kept secretly; Zimbabwe did not allow dual citizenship. He had no idea if the Zimbabwean government believed the press reports or if they still hunted Mwanyisa's assailants. There was nothing for it. He couldn't avoid showing his passport at the gate. He half expected to see his mug shot hanging from a wanted poster on the wall.

Once inside, he waited in a polite British queue.

The woman at the information counter gave the usual reply. She was, grateful for this offer of assistance, but they were unable to accommodate more volunteers at this time.

Stuart muttered to himself.

He persisted until the attendant called the attaché. Maggie Etters, the attaché to the British Ambassador, turned him away. He understood. People everywhere clambered to help, but they didn't need a bunch of unskilled workers endangering the lives of others. Rescue work was hazardous and post disaster unrest created potentially volatile environments. Every well-meaning citizen thought they had something to offer. Stuart needed a resume.

Time for a back door, he thought. Stuart left the building and walked to his rental. He placed a quick call from the parking lot and waited. In a matter of minutes, his cell rang.

"Mr. Hall?" It was Ms. Etters. "I've received a summary of your qualifications," she explained. "A fax just arrived from some influential people in the Zimbabwean political arena. Sorry, I put you off so quickly. Apparently you have extensive experience in logistics from your days with the Selous Scouts."

"Yes, that's right."

"And you're fluent in Shona?"

"Yes, ma'am."

"A logistics station is being arranged as we speak. I'll tell the guards to let you in."

"Thank you." Stuart was relieved to have work to do. "I'll be there in three."

"Good, and Mr. Hall," she paused, "I apologize for turning you away earlier. It's just—"

"I understand, Ms. Etters. Compassion alone doesn't qualify a person for this kind of work."

"Yes, quite so."

He could hear the relief in her voice. She was glad to have him.

#

A piece of plywood rested atop two short filing cabinets. The embassy equipped his crude desk with the most sophisticated communications equipment at their disposal. A total of four telephones—two iridium and two satellite—plus a shortwave for radio contact. The laptop connected to the British High Commissions satellite uplink and someone taped a list of aid and emergency agencies to the desktop. The listed organizations had the capacity to put people on the ground anywhere on the planet within five hours of a natural disaster. They just needed to know where to go.

Nothing like this had ever before been encountered in Africa. The need to find survivors, provide medical relief and stabilize the area required coordination. Stuart had been given a driver's seat.

"Sorry for the crude office." Ms. Etters appeared in the doorway with coffee.

"This is fine." He glanced at the list. "I will need to contact the primary relief agencies first."

"Is there anything else you need?" she asked.

Stuart sat down at the desk and picked up a pen and pad, making notes as he talked. "Yes. I could use four assistants. Preferably people who can get around in German, French, Portuguese, and Afrikaans. It would be helpful if someone was at our disposal who speaks Swazi as well, in case we need to collaborate with the Swazi King. The wonderful thing about a monarch is that they don't have to wait around while everyone asks everyone else for permission to help. I will also need a list of numbers for all the local embassies near the flood zone.

"At the beginning of a disaster, the usual red tape and political posturing almost disappears. We have to capitalize on that cooperation immediately, before the television cameras look the other way and the world begins to forget."

Ms. Etters smiled. "I'll see what I can do."

Chapter 30
New York City
Tuesday, March 16

Vinny sat on the steps outside Travis Sander's apartment, the hood pulled up around his face. Few people were out. It was too damn cold. Vinny daydreamed about normal life. Normal job. Normal family. His own mother had been a plaything to a prominent politician. She made sure Vinny was well connected with the 'family.' Just the wrong kind of family, he guessed. At one time he had even thought to thank her.

He fingered the cardboard cup. Coffee cups provided great cover. A man could sit anywhere with a coffee cup and people thought it was normal. He heard the taxi turn the corner.

About time. He'd been walking around the neighborhood for hours, and he had to piss so bad it hurt. Hurry up, Mr. Sander.

The taxi stopped in front of the building and Travis slipped some bills to his driver. Vinny reached into his coat and slipped off the safety. The city lights rolled off the yellow taxi and Travis crossed the sidewalk. Unsteady. Tipsy.

Good, Vinny thought. All the better. He let go of the handle grip. He could take care of this inside.

Vinny came to his feet as Travis stumbled on the first step. "Whoa, there Mr. Travis. Need a hand?"

Travis looked up at Vinny. "What are you doing here?" he managed.

"Just in the neighborhood for coffee. Looks like you've had a good night." Vinny took Travis's arm and pulled open the apartment door after helping him swipe his key.

"Never expected to see you here." Travis worked his lips carefully to form the words.

Vinny helped him up the stairs and into his apartment.

"Mind if I use your restroom?" he asked.

Travis pointed to the room and sank down on the couch, rubbing his temples. Tried to think.

Vinny stepped behind him and twisted the suppressor onto his .45. He pressed the silencer against the broker's head and pulled the trigger. Travis slumped over.

Vinny dropped a bag of cocaine beside the dead man. The mark of a drug deal gone bad. "Living on the edge, eh?" he whispered.

Then he found the bathroom and relived himself. He left Travis's apartment, locking the door behind him.

Chapter 31
British High Commission
Pretoria, South Africa
March 17

Maggie Etters stopped by the night before and put a sandwich on the desk. Another one, delivered earlier in the day, had gone untouched.

"You need to eat, Mr. Hall," she said.

"Thanks." He handed her a paper. "The latest casualty reports. These numbers mean little at this point. It's too early."

She took the paper, didn't look at it. "I got a call today." She stared at him. "I'm sorry to hear about your loss."

Stuart stopped and looked up. The young woman was attractive in a sensible, British sort of way. She seemed to care. To see into him. Stuart wasn't sure he liked it. He nodded. Said nothing.

"Let me know if you need to talk." She put a hand on his broad shoulder and left.

He worked until he fell asleep at the desk, but woke up around two a.m. Memories of Sheila crept into the silent office. He wept alone, and then ate the sandwich. The bread had gone mushy at the corners and the lettuce wilted. He didn't care.

Grieving was hard work.

Several calls came in during the night from temporary camps. He fell asleep again on a cot Ms. Etters arranged for him. He woke to the sounds of early risers returning to work and tried to remember where he was and why. Then it came back. The dread of grief washed over him.

Get up, he told himself. Keep moving. Keep busy.

He wandered into the hallway and found a bathroom. Stared at himself in the mirror. What a mess. Stuart washed his face and ran wet fingers through his thinning hair.

He needed to walk. Clear his head. It was going to be another long day.

Maggie Etters had given him a pass, and the security guard let him through the gate without question. The half block wall around the British property was topped with black wrought iron. The long row of concrete planters between the sidewalk and the road front stood empty. Not much for decoration, but they served to keep vehicles away from the wall. Cosmetic security considerations.

The March air made Stuart shiver, but he didn't want to go back for a coat. Eventually, he passed the Villa Via Luxury Hotel. Its grand entrance hosted diplomats and VIPS from all over the world. The US embassy was just a few blocks away. He walked aimlessly, lost in his own thoughts, leaving the tragedy of Kariba alone for a few minutes.

Traffic began to pick up. Stuart found his way back to the High Commission. A different guard scrutinized his pass, left him standing at the gate while he returned to the guard shack.

The guard spoke into the phone and glanced at him through the glass. Something was up. For a moment, Stuart wondered if the Zimbabwean government had caught up with him.

The guard returned to the barrier and let Stuart through. "Mr. Hall, Ms. Etters has been looking for you. She has an urgent message." The gate clanged shut behind.

Suddenly, Stuart didn't want to be surrounded by the urgent realities of death and destruction. It felt like too much. He stalled for a moment by the door, deciding if he should go on into the building, but the thought of spending the whole day alone with his own grief pushed him forward. Don't think. Keep busy.

His new mantra.

He passed the building's security scanners and turned down the hallway to Maggie's office.

"Ms. Etters?" Her desk was empty.

A voice called from the hallway. Maggie ran up to him, holding a single piece of paper. "I've been looking all over for you." He noticed her blue eyes wide with excitement.

A familiar dread pressed against him. What now?

"Apparently, you haven't been checking your cell phone. We got a fax early this morning from our UK office." She shoved the paper at him. "Read this."

Stuart stood in the middle of the hallway staring at the paper. He tried to read it again, but the words blurred.

"Ms. Etters, would you—" his voice choked in his throat, "I'm having a hard time making it out."

He noticed tears running down the woman's face. She took the fax from him. Read it aloud.

To: Ms. Maggie Etters / Attaché of the British High Commission
From: Mr. Edwin Caldwell, London Office
Date: 17 March 2007
Subject: Sheila Smith

Please notify a Mr. Stuart Hall that his daughter, Mrs. Sheila Smith, is alive and well and in the company of his wife in Ashbury. He is to contact them at his earliest convenience.

Chapter 32
Zambezi River Disaster Area
Between Zambia and Zimbabwe
March 18

Dr. Gretta crouched by the cot, a hand against the girl's head.

"She doesn't have a fever." Gretta put her hands in her lab coat pockets. "I don't know what the trouble is. She hasn't said a word."

Daniel pulled a simple doll from his rucksack. He'd cut a piece of rope and crafted it into a rag doll, tying off the head and arms with pieces of string. Not bad for his first attempt. Thinking about the girl kept him sane. Human.

A man spoke from the cot next to hers. Bandages covered his head and shoulder. "I think so that she is baTonga," he said in broken English. He addressed the girl in another language. She listened. A flicker in her eyes. A nod. Almost imperceptible.

"Yes, she had been taken to the camp before the water came." The man explained.

"What about her family?" Daniel asked. "Ask about her family?"

The man spoke again, more softly this time. She shook her head, and the man continued. Then paused and sighed. Sadness shrouded the girl. "Her family is late."

The miracle of her survival still astonished the rescuers. The few survivors were talismans of hope. Not hope that more would be found, but hope in the miraculous. A girl saved by clinging to a pink soccer ball. A man spared in the tangle of a tree. An infant found floating in a plastic bucket. Stories became legends. Some, too fantastic to believe.

Daniel held the doll out for the girl, but she ignored it. Her eyes fastened to the earth floor and some other place. He tucked it into the bed next to her and stepped outside. Evening light lay across the canvas village.

Gretta watched him go. She turned back to the man's cot. "If you can, please find out if she has any living relative. We'll need to find someone to take her."

Chapter 33
New York City
Friday, March 19, 2007

Zachary Morgan quietly tracked down all the information he could find about Ciro Michi. The more he found, the more careful he became.

The man had significant political clout in Italy, even though, according to a source, was on the CIA's Watch List. Michi ran one of the largest criminal rings for human trafficking in the Mediterranean. Zachary already knew there were more people in slavery today than at any time in history. Why Michi had been allowed to continue fell outside Zachary's understanding of politics and intrigue.

He sipped a diet soda and placed another call to Travis Sander. It usually took a while for Travis to call back. Travis was, after all, a stockbroker. Since they met on Tuesday, post-its and half napkins from his days on Michi's trail littered Zachary's desk. Most leads fizzed out at dead ends, confidential records or death certificates. Someone had to have been on the ground in Central Africa, helping the dam along.

Scientists were abuzz with logical scenarios for the disaster. And there were many. By most accounts, the dam was inherently unstable. But they missed the obvious, Zachary was sure of it. The more he thought of it, the more he was certain someone facilitated the dam's failure.

He opened *The Wall Street Journal* and scanned the pages. Even a reporter had to stay current on news. Kariba still dominated the front page. It would stay there for a while. But Zachary knew if some presidential aid took her clothes off for her boss, the tragedy would be ancient history. The national attention span grew shorter all the time.

If he was going to break the story, it had to be fast.

He turned a page and stopped cold.

Travis Sander's face stared back at him from the top of a column. He skimmed the article. *Dead. Three days. Gunshot to the head. Drugs. No leads. Police investigating.*

Three days. Zachary's hands suddenly felt clammy. He had seen him three days ago.

Travis never used hard drugs. A classic, mob style murder. The idea chewed its way into his brain like some virulent parasite.

Chapter 34
Johannesburg International Airport
Johannesburg, South Africa
March 20

The Johannesburg International Airport hummed with the work of rescue and recovery. Everywhere, information booths directed pre-registered volunteers who arrived en masse. International peace-time units and military search and rescue teams moved like rivers of order in a sea of chaos. Rescue dogs yipped from their kennels and the melee quickly cooled the starry-eyed idealism of some who had arrived with a desire to help but no idea what to do. The Red Cross and other non-governmental organizations mounted semi-coordinated efforts, but the confused masses in the terminal drew a more accurate picture of the international response.

South African soldiers armed with Israeli-issue automatic weapons, patrolled the mob. Wide-eyed volunteers from an Oklahoma church took pictures of the burly, armed men in khaki. Those who had been to Africa before didn't notice the soldiers.

Stuart tried all morning to find Daniel. Frustrated and excited, he stood on a seat in arrivals lounge at Gate Five, watching still more passengers disgorge from the Boeing 747.

Above the chaos, a single voice screamed out, "Daddy!" Stuart leapt from the seat, pushed his way through people toward the voice. Duffel bags and carts materialized before him, but he pushed on until he swept Sheila into his arms and held her fast. He sobbed then, like he hadn't before. His own dam broke, and he sat down on the floor, holding Sheila among the crowds and baggage. Crying and laughing and rocking his daughter. Kathy joined them.

Happiness in the midst of chaos. People gathered around. Watching, smiling. Something to celebrate.

The Oklahomans snapped more pictures.

Chapter 35
Pretoria, South Africa
British High Commission
March 22

Stuart tossed the pen into the mess on his desk. "It is like looking for a needle in a haystack."

"Daddy, why can't you just send a picture out and ask if anyone has seen him?" Sheila spent most of her time in the office with her father. She felt safer just being close to him.

"Luv, I have to be careful. Until things settle down in Zimbabwe, there may be people looking for him. He is the only one of us we know that Mwanyisa connected with Gideon Chipinduka. I don't want to put him in danger," Stuart answered.

"Why would they be looking for you if they think you're dead?" she asked.

"True, but if his picture starts turning up, they'll figure out he's still around."

"What are we going to do?" Sheila chewed at her nails. She'd lost weight in spite of the pregnancy. Stuart worried about her.

"You are going to take care of yourself and the little one. I am going to keep trying. Remember, Danny probably isn't using his real name. I don't know what name he is using, wherever he is." He sighed. "If people start asking around for Daniel Smith, he might think the Zimbabwean government is after him. That doesn't exactly make someone want to identify himself."

Tears rolled down Sheila's cheeks. "I feel like I'm losing him all over again. Daddy, I don't think I can bear it."

Stuart pawed through the papers until he found a number. He pulled out his cell and tried again. He'd already left several text messages. So many cell towers had been affected by the regional black outs that many areas remained out of service.

The Rat made a small fortune flying emergency personnel into areas most other pilots wouldn't dream of attempting. He worked around the clock. Stuart listened to it ring. Still nothing.

Sheila watched. Suddenly Stuart came to attention in his chair.

"Rat?" He fairly shouted into the phone.

Static dogged the line and Stuart pressed his finger into his free ear, struggling to hear.

"I'm trying to find Danny. Where did you take him after you left?"

Stuart screwed his eyes tight shut. Trying to understand, couldn't make out the words.

"Check your text messages and get back to me," Stuart shouted. The connection failed.

He slumped back into his chair and shook his head. "I have no idea if he could even hear me." He closed the phone and dropped it on his desk. He looked at his daughter. "He is our best lead, Sheila. I'm not going to give up."

She walked to the window overlooking the Commission's grounds. "What if he doesn't want to be found?" she asked.

"What are you talking about?"

"I walked out on him, Daddy. I didn't want him to go ahead with what you were planning. I was afraid."

He walked to her, put his hand on her shoulder. Her body was tense. "Sheila I told him to let you go."

"You did what?" she was confused. Betrayed.

Stuart pressed on. "If you had stayed in the country, you would have put him in more danger. If they had caught you, they would have wanted him in exchange. He would have traded himself; I have no doubt. If that happened, you would never have seen him again."

"Why didn't you just tell me?" she struggled through fresh angry tears.

"Sheila, I don't expect you to understand. I know you've never believed in my wars. But this was bigger than our farm, or you or Daniel." His voice dropped to a whisper. "The entire country was dying under the strangle hold of that monster. When Daniel told me you were upset and threatening to leave, I told him to let you go off to England. I knew he would come and find you."

She stared hard into his face, shrugged off his embrace and walked out of the room.

Stuart returned to his desk and sank into his chair. He was tired. It had been almost a week since Sheila came 'back to life'. Yet, he would still wake up sobbing and Kathy would have to remind him his daughter was alive. He stared at the phone.

"Come on, Rat. I need to hear from you." Stuart muttered.

Chapter 36
Somewhere in central Mozambique
March 22

The Rat banked hard, squinting against the sun as he skimmed the dried mud flat. The beauty of this flood, he determined, was that it created lots of flat smooth places for airplanes. He studied the ground for signs of wet mud and came in again. This time his tires touched down on the flats. The plane bounced once and settled into the landing.

The Skymaster slowed, and The Rat taxied around a half-buried elephant carcass protruding from the surface like a bizarre modern sculpture. Only the back legs and tail extended above dried mud, bloated and reeking from days in the sun.

Joey Greer opened the window in his door and killed the engines. The smell was staggering.

"There you go, ma'am. Welcome to the flush zone." He pointed to the flat smear extending as far as they could see.

He removed his safety belt and pushed open the door to exit the sweltering cabin. He stood in the wing's shade. "Nothing but mud and death."

The reporter climbed from her seat and vomited by the wheel of the plane. The Rat smiled at the sound. "Got a little bumpy up there for you, eh?" He chuckled and pulled a cigar from his breast pocket. "Yup, if the queasies don't get you, the smell down here will certainly do the trick." He lit a match and touched it to the end of the cigar. "This will help."

"Sorry," she managed, "I've never been a good traveler in small planes." She wiped her mouth on a tissue from her handbag. "You'd think with my work, I'd have gotten over it by now. No such luck." She clicked a few photos of the elephant. "Is this what it's like everywhere?" she asked.

"Yup. Everywhere. Elephants turned on their heads. Even in Madagascar. They've never seen elephants over there." He blew smoke in front of his face, trying to get rid of the smell. "Elephants, buffalo, even giraffe. All kinds of creatures on their beaches. Like a big, dead zoo."

Greer sat down on the tire. "I wouldn't be surprised if the animals of Africa start washing up in Perth."

"Perth?" she asked, not following.

"Australia."

She put a piece of gum in her mouth and walked away from the plane, snapping pictures and speaking notes into a digital recorder. It was too big to capture.

"Remember," he called after her, "no pictures of me or my plane."

"I remember," she replied.

The Rat pulled a cell from his pocket. Two messages waiting. I must have flown past an active tower on my way in, he thought. He flicked ash from his cigar and thumbed through the messages.

Chapter 37
Lusaka, Zambia
March 23

Dr. Gideon Chipinduka stood up to the studio microphone.

Gideon dreamed of this moment. The days he sat hungry and alone in prison had given him time to craft and memorize every single word. The Zambian BBC correspondent gave him the go-ahead, and Gideon began. His address would be broadcast via shortwave, television and YouTube when the power was on.

"People of Zimbabwe, my name is Gideon Chipinduka. Although I was the one you chose at our last election, I was unlawfully imprisoned by the illigitimate leader of this country, Cedric Mwanyisa. While I have been in jail, the economic and political condition of Zimbabwe has plummeted. The safety, productivity and economy of Zimbabwe suffer deeply. Cedric Mwanyisa determined to profit himself and the vultures who gathered around him to feed on the people of Zimbabwe. Now, our money is worth so little it is used to start fires, and our women are afraid of those who have been emboldened by the lawlessness of Mwanyisa's tyranny.

"Our country descended from people who knew the value of this land and were willing to pay the full price for it. Yet, we have now become a nation of bystanders, watching the flood of greed, the rot of caprice, and the terror of fear paralyze and overwhelm us. At night we see the hyena's green eyes watching our children. In the daylight, we see death birds circling, waiting for them to die.

"People of Zimbabwe, the time for watching is over.

"In conjunction with international lawyers, I have brought charges against the *former* President, Cedric Mwanyisa, for crimes committed against the people of Zimbabwe. After his recovery, he will stand trial for the suffering he invited into our houses, our villages, and our tribes. With full backing from our military, I have personally contacted the previous members of Mwanyisa's cabinet, demanding their resignation.

"In addition, I have appointed an emergency cabinet of ministers to operate in the intermediate. In three months, Zimbabwe will hold *free* elections monitored by representatives of member nations of the Southern African Development Community. These nations have not only pledged to monitor and assist in our elections, but have joined hands with us to help pull Zimbabwe out of this ditch."

Gideon paused and removed the glasses from his face. His eyes focused on the people beyond the camera.

"Printed on our coins are pictures of the Great Zimbabwe Ruins. This ancient site is a reminder of a long and powerful history. Unfortunately, the Ruins have become more than a symbol of our past, they have become a picture of our present. Our former greatness is forgotten. We are nothing but a memory of the past.

"But I have not forgotten what Zimbabwe was. I have not forgotten what she could be again."

He stopped. Paused to collect himself.

"Today is the beginning. Join with me in asking God to stand at the door of our tomb and declare, 'Zimbabwe, come forth.'"

A red light appeared on the studio wall. Gideon wiped his face and glasses with a handkerchief.

Davison Chuma entered the studio room and extended his hand.

"Well done, Mr. President."

Chapter 38
Johannesburg, South Africa
March 24

Civil engineer, Arturo Esposito, traveled to South Africa to watch his work and celebrate with Cedric Mwanyisa. He planned on traveling to Zimbabwe after The Southern African Development Community convened. All completely off line, of course.

When they first made the arrangements, Arturo asked where he would go through customs, but the old man laughed. Mwanyisa was the President. The law. The chief customs agent. Clearly he did what he wanted. A private jet would fly Arturo inconspicuously into the country.

Now, that all seemed like a long time ago.

Newspapers littered the floor of his motel room. A thin light pushed in around drawn curtains, competing with the television's blue glow. He flipped constantly through channels, hunting for news of the president. Surely, if the man had lived two weeks, he was going to make it. If he made it, the reconstruction contract the dictator signed would be valid and Arturo would be fabulously wealthy.

He leaned over yet another order of Chinese take-out from across the street. His chopsticks fished out the last lo mein noodle from the cardboard carton. For two weeks, Arturo had nearly gone mad with the waiting. He considered going down to the hospital and inquiring after the president himself, yet he risked enough traveling to South Africa in the first place. The trip was purely reactive. He could do nothing for the man. Besides, Arturo felt safer being further away from Ciro Michi.

The entire scheme depended on one thin black signature.

The Kariba flood dominated headlines. He anticipated being able to gloat as he watched the news, but his whole life was bound up in that one black line. The prognosis for Mwanyisa was still up for grabs and no change meant no news. The newscasters grew tired of reporting Mwanyisa *still* in critical condition.

The real stories followed the Zambezi River and Arturo lived with the constant imagery of destruction, loss and deprivation.

His work.

At first, the pictures hadn't bothered him. After all, he expected it to be like this. Planned for it. Mostly.

He hadn't expected the Cahora Bassa dam to crumble so easily. Likely the spillway basin already suffered erosion, weakening the dam's anchor point in the riverbed. The whole disaster was magnificent, he mused. His initial elation shattered with news of the attack on Mwanyisa.

"Live, you old bastard. Live," Arturo muttered. He'd recited the words a thousand times. Once, he even tried praying, but the incongruity was too much for him, and he ended his prayer with a simple, "Never mind."

He nibbled the end off a fortune cookie and pulled at the ribbon of paper inside. Read it aloud. "A surprise awaits." Arturo snorted and crumbled the paper.

If Mwanyisa died, he could never return to Italy. Ciro Michi only forgave the dead. Arturo shoved aside the covers on the unmade bed and propped up a pillow. The smell of stale cigarette smoke lingered. Another round of banal commercials interrupted his vigil. His teeth felt horrible and his face itched with the new beard that began to fill in. He took another sip of the water he'd purchased from Mr. Fung then pushed a soy packet aside to reach the remote.

He changed the channel.

Still nothing.

Exhaustion swept over him. His eyes felt heavy, but he determined to keep listening. His life was on the line as well. This wasn't supposed to turn out this way.

The television screen swam; Arturo shook his head. It felt as if his body were pressed into the mattress. Must be more tired than he realized.

He heard the sound of water running somewhere far away. He pried open his eyes, the room floated. Must have been a bad batch of noodles.

Then he smelled a faint fragrance he recognized, but couldn't place. So tired. He looked up. A woman. What was she doing here? How did she get in? She spoke, but he couldn't hear. Probably a dream.

He felt hands grip his legs and arms. A black face and the woman. Not white, but olive. Italian? He couldn't move.

He tried to speak, nothing came out.

Strange. He tried to reason it out, but thought stalled in his brain; it irritated him.

A hood was drawn over his head and pulled tight. Hands lifted him, dragged him across the floor.

Chapter 39
Hospital
Johannesburg, South Africa
March 24

Cedric Mwanyisa looked smaller than he had in decades. Excess flesh had melted off his frame, leaving his face drawn and gaunt. Bandages worked their way around multiple wires attached to adhesive sensors on his chest. Live feeds linked to monitors at the nurses' station down the hall. The artificial respirator breathed out a steady rhythm for the comatose patient. Occasionally, an automatic IV dispenser growled. A television, mounted to the wall, chattered out the news.

The constant beep of Mwanyisa's heart monitor argued with the regular tick of a room clock. Military police from the South African Defense Force stood their posts outside the door. Armed with 9 mm BXP submachine guns, protecting what was left of the old man's life.

A nurse checked the clipboard in the bin outside his room. She flashed her badge and a smile to the guards as she passed. She held a syringe of what appeared to be antibiotic. It was, in fact, a special gift delivered in time for rounds.

"Good morning, Mr. President, its nurse Patty. It is a beautiful day out there." She pulled the curtains to let in the sunlight. "You've not been out carousing last night, have you?" She rambled on, talking to the man like she did with all her patients. She lifted the sheet at the foot of the bed and noted the fluid levels in the catheter bag before replacing it with a fresh one.

Then she injected the contents of her syringe into the IV port and adjusted the drip rate. "Here's some breakfast. Not quite like a coffee, but it should help with the healing." She entered a few notes on her chart before leaving the room.

Overhead, the newscaster said something about Zimbabwe, and the screen flicked to a close up of Gideon Chipinduka. The voice mingled with sounds of monitors and respirators.

Cedric Mwanyisa opened his eyes.

Then the beeping stopped and an alarm sounded at the nurse's desk.

Chapter 40
Crocodile Sanctuary
Outside Johannesburg, South Africa

Monet Botha made his final round. The last of the school groups finally left. Crocodiles were far more predictable, he thought. One could always count on them to be ugly, mean, and hungry. Botha locked up the nursery after giving the incubator a cursory examination. Even crocodiles are cute when they're little.

It never made sense. Sometimes the smallest, mild mannered teachers had their students well in line. Then some brash, bullying, dried-out-crust of an old bear would have students running all over the place with absolutely no control.

The sign on the gate read: '*Children must remain with an adult at all times. Crocodiles are dangerous animals.*' Botha sighed. Nobody read the sign. When he took this job, he thought he would be working with animals.

I guess that part was true, he thought. Funny. The most dangerous animals were allowed to walk around, and the rest were kept in cages.

Children were cute but entirely unpredictable. He had given today's group the grand, field-trip experience. Bilbo cooperated perfectly. The sanctuary's oldest croc leapt almost entirely out of the water to reach the chicken he dangled overhead on the pike. The overspray splashed a few of the kids closest to the railing. It was magnificent.

But one cheeky little brat said, "Agh, Mineer, I already saw that on the television."

Why do I do this? Botha wondered.

On the other hand, when he took them into the sanctuary's nature house, the children were completely fascinated with the crocodile skeleton. They listened with horrified attention to his lecture. A croc, he told them, could catch a bird in flight with a side strike of over 250 kilometers per hour. Teeth as long as fingers. After twenty-four hours, a croc forgets he has eaten. They listened to the list of facts, but were bored with Bilbo.

He didn't get it.

Every day, he would pull out the same, wiggling baby croc from the nursery for show and tell. The kids loved the perfectly shaped reptile with unmoving eyes and light green scales not yet hardened by Africa's sun. But Botha knew that when it got large enough, the same creature would happily pull him by some dangling leg out of a boat and drag him in circles underwater until the bubbles stopped. Then it would wedge him under a submerged branch, so he'd cooperate while the creature tore off pieces of his body. Botha shuddered. At least crocodiles were predictable.

Botha locked the main gate and stuffed the keys in his pocket. He climbed into his car and headed home. His wife was a schoolteacher. She would understand.

#

The drug wore off slowly. Arturo Esposito had no idea how long he had been out. Hours? Days? However long, he was now fully awake. Awake and aware that everything had gone entirely wrong. Michi's people found him.

His stomach and legs felt weak with fear. *The fish were always hungry.* He could still smell the woman, but his captors did not speak. Their silence only increased the awful feeling in his stomach. He felt the vehicle slow and turn. He didn't know where they were going, but he was certain he didn't want to get there.

105

Fear and motion sickness conspired against him and Esposito vomited. The hood over his head held the sticky wet mess against the side of his face and it dripped down inside the collar of his shirt. It made him feel less human, less in control. His bowels threatened.

The van stopped. Arturo's legs trembled involuntarily. "Please," he tried again, "I am a rich man. Free me, and you will never regret it. Michi wants me alive."

No response. He was begging for his life. The van door opened; he was pulled roughly from the vehicle. His numb hands ached from being bound too tightly behind his back.

Bolt cutters snapped through a padlock, and the party let themselves in through the side gate. Arturo eyes bulged, fighting to see through his hood. Here and there pinpricks of light penetrated the weave, but he could see nothing. Darkness and the smell of vomit surrounded him.

Arturo heard the sound of another padlock being cut and the rattle of chain. Another gate. Chain link. His captors shoved him from behind.

"Take off his trousers," the woman said. Matter of fact, as if she were ordering an extra pound of cheese sliced at a deli counter.

"What are you doing?" he demanded. Esposito grew frantic. Hands yanked open his trousers and someone kicked his feet from under him. His trousers were dragged from his legs, taking a shoe with them. A man chuckled at his silk boxers.

"Hold him down." The woman again.

"My name is Colette and you are just in time for dinner." Strong hands pinned him to the cold ground. She took a razor blade and made a deep vertical cut down the length of his shin, blade scraping against bone. Esposito screamed.

"Good," the woman said, "keep screaming. Bilbo likes that."

"What do you want with me?" he blubbered.

"Mr. Esposito. We don't want anything, but he might."

"Who? Please, take the bag off my head."

"Bilbo."

"Who is Bilbo?" he asked. The leg was on fire. Blood soaked into his sock.

She ripped the hood away. Esposito stared around him. A black man and the woman. She was beautiful. Had he seen her before?

"Who is Bilbo?" he asked.

"Bilbo is the River God." Colette pointed down the grassy bank at the black water. She flicked on a flashlight illuminating a pair of deep red eyes. "That is Bilbo."

Arturo's face twisted in horror and he began to gag.

A few feet from the water's edge an iron ring hung from a thick post planted deep in the ground. The man dragged Arturo to the picket, looped a chain through his handcuffs and fastened it to the ring with a padlock. He dangled the keys in front of Arturo's face then dropped them at his feet. Arturo immediately lunged for it, but the binding bit harshly into his wrists and held him fast.

"Bag him again," the woman said.

"No." Esposito tried to resist, but the man punched him low and hard and the hood was drawn again over his head. The fabric, still sticky from his own vomit, clung to his face. Esposito shook his head frantically, trying to get it off.

"Mr. Esposito," the woman spoke. "This is what is going to happen." She talked as if delivering a mini-lecture to a naughty child. "You will probably dislocate at least one of your shoulders before Bilbo ever leaves the water. And he will leave the water. The smell of blood, you see, makes him hungry. Unfortunately, Bilbo doesn't have cutting teeth, you understand, just long spikes. He will grab you by a leg, probably breaking a bone and try to pull you in. When he does, both your shoulders will certainly dislocate. The pain will be extraordinary. But Bilbo won't be able to drown you in the water, so he will have to tear you apart on land. He's quite capable, though.

"Scream, if you like. He won't mind. In the morning, when the school children come for a tour, they will find a pair of tailored Italian trousers draped over the chain link fence and, perhaps, a single hand left dangling from the post.

"While you are waiting to die, Mr. Esposito, you can think about what you are going to say to the Honorable Cedric Mwanyisa when you meet him in hell."

"Why are you doing this?" Arturo asked. A stupid question.

He felt the woman rest her hand on his chest. "Ciro Michi said I should be creative."

Arturo heard them turn and walk back up the bank, leaving him half-naked and trembling at the post. A chain rattled through the gate and a padlock clicked into place.

Chapter 41
Peacock Farm
Zimbabwe
May, 2007

Stuart turned onto the familiar drive. Grass had over-grown the fenced meadows on either side of the farm lane. Kathy and Sheila sat in the back seat, each lost in their own memories. So much had happened since they fled in the middle of the night. The farm belonged to another life. Another story. Still, in spite of the tall grass and empty meadows, everything was familiar. The turns in the lane. The trees. The boulders seemingly dropped at random across the land.

Stuart stopped to inspect the bridge. A few timbers had been pilfered, but most remained intact. He picked his way over the gaps. In the center, he stopped again and killed the engine.

Iridescent dragonflies fled like sparks from the water's edge. Butterflies lolled in the mud along the creek bank and a purple gallinule crept among the reeds further down, flicking its tail feathers as it walked. Sheila once played in the water here on hot days, full of life and chatter about mud pies and water bugs and pretty stones.

That was a far-away time. Stuart wondered if the carefree happy girl would ever be back.

He restarted the engine and drove up toward the farmhouse. Weeds had over taken the packed stone drive. The house, his wedding present to Kathy, lay in ruins. The stone and plaster walls still stood, but empty burned-out windows stared with blackened eyes. The entire roof collapsed in the blaze. A kind of calm hung over the place, as if it knew the worst was over.

The fire had been a parting gift from the man who had once been Mwanyisa's friend and was now in jail. Kathy leaned forward and patted Stuart's shoulder. "It was about time we downsized, anyway," she said, trying to hide her own sadness.

He got out and walked toward the shell of their former life. A few charred timbers outlined where the roof had been. He stepped through the doorway and into the room. Broken bits and pieces from kitchen cupboards lay strewn about the living room floor. Whoever torched the place had trashed it first.

The fireplace stood boldly in the center of a grand room. Stuart built it to be seen from both sides, so they could watch the flames dance from the dining room as well. But now, the dressed stone mantle stood under an open sky.

Houses can be rebuilt, Stuart thought, but lives? That was another matter, altogether.

Sheila had withdrawn into isolation. She performed the required functions of daily life, and her belly kept growing. But the loss of Daniel left a rift in her heart that seemed beyond repair.

The days had grown into weeks. Then months. There was no word. No closure. Nothing. Satellite imagery displayed Africa's destruction, but satellites didn't pick up wounded hearts. Sheila stopped asking about Daniel. Stuart stopped reporting that he heard nothing. Flood recovery operations were still in full force, but Stuart handed over his post to others so they could go home.

Zimbabwe's elections stood a few weeks away, but it would be years until the country recovered from its previous leadership. The people were ready. A kind of buoyancy mingled with the smell of cooking fires.

Stuart just stood for a while, staring at the cold old ashes of his past. Somehow, he had expected some things to stay the same. Silently, he tried to reorder his expectations.

Looking through the burned out doorway he could see the grass surrounding the wreckage of their home. Its yellow-green spires danced as wind played overhead.

Stuart cocked his head to one side. Heard a sound. Maybe nothing. Then he heard it again. He knew it. He was sure. Hope fluttered in his tired chest. He looked up, face to the sky.

Kathy stood in the doorway. "What is it, luv?"

"Don't you hear that?" he asked.

"What are you talking—" she started, but Stuart held a finger to her lips. The sound grew quickly. Whatever it was, traveled fast.

Stuart started running. A Cessna Skymaster exploded into the sky, flying just above the tree tops. A wave of prop wash pressed the grass down and stirred up ashes in the old house. The twin boom plane was unmistakable.

Sheila looked to her father. Her eyes wild and green and afraid.

"Get in!" he shouted.

Their doors slammed. Gears ground into place and tires tore at the gravel drive. The truck jerked over the rutted track. Sheila held the little mound of her stomach as they jolted along, her face drawn and pale.

They passed the workers' village. It stood empty. The generator house with its tin roof was unchanged. A broken gate clung awkwardly to its post. Stuart smashed through it toward a back meadow that sometimes served as an airstrip.

Surely The Rat had seen their truck.

Stuart stopped the vehicle at the field's edge and pulled the key. They got out, ears straining. The Cessna disappeared. Puffy clouds lazed in the blue expanse, but nothing else.

Sheila bit her lip and leaned against the hood to steady herself.

The sound returned. A far away hum, growing quickly. The plane reappeared above the trees. The pilot feathered the prop and the plane eased down on the meadow. He killed the engine to keep the propeller from being damaged in the grass; then slipped it into a turn and stopped.

The Rat stepped out and nodded in their direction. He held the door. A black girl jumped down beside him. Another man tumbled out behind her, running as soon as he hit the ground.

Stuart heard Sheila choke out a sob. She pushed away from the truck. They met in the middle. Daniel swept her up and around in circles. Abruptly he stopped. Aware of her belly. He knelt down, put his ear against her stomach and held their child.

The Tonga girl drew up behind Daniel. Her eyes were wide and shy.

Daniel turned. "Her name is Gift."

Sheila held out a hand and drew the child into an embrace.

Other books by this author include:

The Zambezi Chronicles
      The Contract*
      Critical Fault*
      Cover of Darkness

And

The Moderator Series
      The Moderator
      The Coma
      Grid Lock

Audio available from Audible.com or iTunes.com.

On Facebook at www.facebook.com/dwightkoppbooks

On the web at www.dwightkopp.com

Acknowledgements

Special thanks to Doreen (Doe) Kopp, and Martha and Jay Squaresky for editing assistance. All remaining errors are still my fault. Thanks to Captain Derek Reimer who tried to help me speak 'satellite.' Any lingering inaccuracies are also mine.

About the Author

Dwight Kopp lived (mostly) in Zambia until he was thirteen. His fondest memories include listening to the sound of elephants raiding the peanut fields as he drifted off to sleep. He now lives and writes in Lancaster County where he married the woman of his dreams. They have five (amazing) children.

www.ingramcontent.com/pod-product-compliance
Lightning Source LLC
Chambersburg PA
CBHW072008170626
46813CB00005B/2062